SECRET TERRY

By Horatio Quan and Daphne McGuire

ISBN 978-1-7386776-3-4

Dedicated to Valeria Quan

Special thanks to our editor Vladimir Schmuck

Table of Contents

Part 1:

COLD CUT

Prologue:
A Meaty Conversation

Dick Richard was the best in the business. At least, he thought so. With that self-assurance in mind and without knocking, he boldly opened the door to his latest client's office and entered. The décor reflected the personality of its owner, powerful manly wood grains and granite alongside plush velvety draping. Seeing his usually intimidating client seated behind the large walnut desk, Dick nonetheless confidently sauntered up to the sturdy piece of furniture and whipped it out, flopping it down on the smooth lacquered surface. There was an audible thud and the various glass decanters and colorful bottles of alcohol on the sideboard rattled, the liquids inside quivering. It was 11 inches long and over 3 inches thick, looking well-worn as if from extensive handling, and so engorged it appeared ready to burst. The man sitting at the desk lightly licked his lips and stared at it with avid interest, a covetous and almost nostalgic look in his eyes.

"Here's what I've got," Dick said to the man. "I think you'll be well pleased."

The man at the desk reached out with a strong, hairy hand and gently stroked it before grasping it tightly and picking it up – a manila folder with

CONFIDENTIAL stamped on it, stuffed full with page after page of letter sized paper. In addition to the previously mentioned dimensions, it was also 8.5 inches wide. He placed the file back down on the desk, almost reverently, and went to open it. Instead, he hesitated a moment and withdrew his hands, looking up to regard the man in front of him. Dick Richard, Private Investigator, looking as grizzled and hard-boiled as a cheese sandwich with egg. Despite the frumpy rumpled trench coat and overly large hat pulled down over his eyes, the man at the desk could tell just by looking at him that Dick Richard's reputation as a guy who could get it done was no exaggeration – the size of his package in front of him attested to that.

"Tell me what you've found," the man at the desk said to his hired detective.

Dick shifted in his seat, adjusting his pants. "It took me a long time, but I think I finally found your guy. He's a slippery shadow, a ghost's whisker, a wisp of a whisper. If I've got it right, in terms of covert operations, especially in the world of corporate espionage, he's not just the best in the business; he's nine of the top ten entries on the list. Trade secrets, hidden bank accounts, cutting edge unpatented technology, compromising materials, a bit of light assassination, he does it all. He's an independent contractor, well, he might be as many as a dozen independent contractors, available only through the dark web. I've managed to trace him to pretty much every country in Europe. His methodology varies, but one consistency is he seems to operate undercover by actually working for the targets he hits. And he takes that part seriously, every place I think I've tied him to attests that he's the finest employee they've ever had, impeccable work habits, they'd hire him back in a second. Usually he disappears without suspicion, without a trace, and with a great reference. It took me forever to track him down, I don't think I'm bragging when I say that no one else has ever even come close to putting these hits all together and tying them to one person. Most of what he's done is never made public at all."

"An impressive resume to be sure."

"The breadcrumb you gave me was barely a starting point, and this guy is tight, airtight. Took a miracle to take the next step, but nonetheless I'm certain this is the guy you've been searching for. And beyond that, I'm certain he's exactly what you need for your little problem."

"So how'd he slip up?" asked the man at the desk.

Dick eyed his client, sizing up his large but not fat frame, the thick but not off-putting body hair he could see on his arms and peeking out from his slightly too unbuttoned shirt. "He got distracted. It seems our man has a predilection for getting involved romantically, or at least sexually, wherever he goes. Usually he's so good that he wouldn't leave behind a speck of evidence, but on his last job he got too involved, spilled his coffee a bit. Must have been something special to trip him up. Once I found that thread, I started pulling and putting the pieces together and made myself a sweater."

The man at the desk smiled slyly, pretending to understand the metaphors. "Excellent. Now, tell me about the man himself."

"His full name is Terry O'Broadside. No middle name, or if he does have one it's so secret that not even I could find out what it was."

"I thought you were the best in the business?"

"I am, but so is he. You know, in his line of business."

"And his full first name is actually just Terry? Not Terrence?"

"No, definitely not Terrence, that I'm sure about."

"Hmm." This seemed to displease Dick's client a great deal. "Very well, continue."

"He's a peak athlete, once the most highly recruited handball player in the country. Starred in university, everyone thought he'd turn pro before he quit the team and vanished after graduating with a degree in business. Minored in fashion design and he was president of the gardening club. He'd be 30 this year and no one's sure what he's been doing since then. Until now that is."

"Let's get to the meat of it. What makes him tick? How does he pick his jobs? What makes him so good?"

"Well, he's certainly no Robin Hood. He commands as high a price as can be found in his line of work. But it seems he only takes on jobs targeting those you might consider the worst of the liverwurst, the cream of the corrupt. As I had started mentioning, his usual modus operandi is to take on a low-profile job with extensive access to sensitive information. Sometimes something like an office administrator, an executive assistant, or most often as a highly effective and eminently competent..."

Chapter 1:
Male Secretary

Secretary work was no joke and Terry never treated it as such, even it wasn't his real job. If anyone were to have looked into the usually securely locked corner office that Terry was in, they would have seen Terry bent over, firm buns pressing tightly against his immaculately well pressed suit pants, professionally working away at the sort of things secretaries did. He was rifling through the bottom drawer of a filing cabinet, his perfectly manicured fingers nimbly dancing through the papers and files. Of course, no one did spot him in there – Terry was that good. The fact that it was midnight would have been suspicious if anyone had though.

He straightened up, having satisfied himself that he had left no stone unturned and no burger unflipped. A small smile dimpled his face, his just the right amount of stubble barely hiding the deepening cleft in his strong chin. "Another day, another dollar," he thought to himself as he tucked the paper files he had copied into his smart leather briefcase. A professional piece of art from end to end, this job. In his mind, this would more than make up for his... mild error he had made on his previous job. His first error ever, and in his private world that had shaken him to his foundation. Not a huge problem professionally; he'd had to abandon that online profile entirely despite fulfilling most of what he'd been employed to do, just out of principle. On a personal level though... best not to think about that. Today was a good day. He gave his briefcase a friendly pat, closed and locked the door behind him, and left his current place of work for the last time.

Whistling lightly, he made his way down to the lobby via the staircase. They had even thrown him a little goodbye party this afternoon. The temp worker who had so quickly made himself indispensable. No one ever suspected that a smartly dressed, impossibly well-groomed male secretary could be up to anything nefarious in the office. Even in the corridors of the most powerful corporations, his lithe, masculine figure and attractive, mildly effeminate facial features kept the eyes of any onlookers exactly where he wanted them, and away from any extracurricular activities he might be up to in their databases.

Opening the door at the bottom of the stairs, he surveyed the scene in front of him – nothing unusual, unless of course you counted the two new burly private enforcement goon types standing in front of the only exit, both with rugged beards and suspiciously large bulges in their pants. They were either carrying firearms or greatly enjoying one another's company. Were they waiting for him? Terry checked his own bulge, which while no less impressive was unfortunately just his penis. It seemed impossible to him that he'd slipped up and alerted anyone as to what he was doing on this job, not with how careful he'd been after the debacle that was his last job. So he hadn't considered arming himself or the possibility of running into any obstacles on his way out. Still, this wasn't the first time he'd been in a tight spot with a couple of big tough men. He intended to squeeze out of this one too, and strode out confidently, nodding at the two men as he approached.

"How are you gentlemen?" he asked in passing. Out of the corner of his eye, through his long luxuriant eyelashes, he saw the two of them nod to one another.

"Evening sir," one said, turning and reaching down towards his own crotch.

"Going to be one of those nights, is it?" Terry thought to himself. He gave his butt-cheeks a momentary clench, feeling immediately reassured that all was in place and would go well. He ran a hand through his thick blonde hair that just barely reached his ideally balanced eyebrows to ensure it wouldn't get in his way, even though not a strand was out of place. To say that Terry was fastidious in his self-care would be wildly understating the situation – personal hygiene was more of a way of life for Terry than a habit.

Quick as a flash, Terry turned and issued a smooth karate chop right into the first goon's throat. Terry's well-moisturized hand connected solidly, and he felt the man's windpipe collapse. The goon doubled over, his hand still down his pants reaching for his gun. Terry raised his leg high above his head, then dropped it swiftly down onto the bent-over thug's head, knocking him out cold. This also had the somewhat unexpected result of pulling the goon's pants down around his legs. Terry looked up, unperturbed by this development, his silken complexion mildly flushed pink on his cheeks from the exertion. The sight of his colleague's exposed rear caught the second goon off-guard, but he was quicker than his partner, still managing to withdraw his piece from where it was concealed in his pants.

Thinking quickly, Terry breathed in deeply through his nostrils, biting his full pink lower lip, and threw his beautiful briefcase directly at the second goon. The goon fumbled his gun and caught the case, only to be hit directly in the chest by it as Terry aimed a flying dropkick right into the other side of it, sending him tumbling. The goon cracked his head on the floor and slid away along the ground, seemingly unconscious, Terry's briefcase landing beside him.

Terry heard a muffled yelp and noticed a typical mall-cop type night security guard poking his head up above the lobby reception desk. The guard quickly ducked back down, and Terry could hear the sound of someone frantically hammering at a hidden alarm button. The two he'd incapacitated weren't working with the usual building security employees then. The metal security grate started to descend, and Terry knew it was time to go. He glanced briefly at his abandoned briefcase, overturned next to the sprawled-out goon. No time to grab it. Letting out a light sigh, Terry executed a perfect somersaulting roll, slid under the gate, and walked briskly to where his car was parked nearby.

He remotely started the vehicle and admired it as he approached. The new fully electric Nissan Cube, just released this year, his one area of vanity. All the convenience and storage of a van with the footprint of a compact car. Terry polished every inch of it daily and he knew he'd find the interior spotless. Owning this car sometimes attracted a little too much sexual attention when he took it out for a night on the town, but it was well worth it to feel its boxy form heroically smashing through the wind when he took it for a spin on the Autobahn. He hopped in and pulled out, gliding down the street.

Terry knew he had nothing to worry about. He had already scrubbed the building's security cameras remotely from his phone. But two jobs in a row now that hadn't exactly gone as planned. That was absurd. Who were those goons waiting for him in the lobby, and how had they known he was there? They didn't seem to be regular employees of the building. No one should have been able to connect him to that briefest, narrowest exposure caused by his quick exit from his previous job. Was he really losing his touch then, or was there something more to it? Did it have anything to do with the person who had caused the terrible chain of events that had happened on his last job? That last job… how it all gone so wrong? And would it keep coming back to haunt him? No way of knowing now, he'd have to think about it.

All in all, though, not a bad few weeks and this night could have gone a lot worse. Another successful hit, done and done well despite the last-minute hiccup. It was a shame about the briefcase. It was no knock-off and he had to go to great trouble and expense to replace them every time he lost one. Terry was very particular. Still, he would be well compensated for the past month's work, culminating in tonight's escape. Abandoning a briefcase, especially justified through its part in his cool ninja kick, was after all a tried-and-true method of convincing anyone after him that he hadn't made it out with anything of value. He clenched his buns together again, feeling the familiar contours of his well-hidden data drive safely between them, like a data drive sandwich. Another tried and true technique that Terry was fond of. The paper files in his briefcase would have been nice, Terry loved stationary, but he had of course digitized everything. All that was left was to submit it to his client.

Secret agent work was no joke either, but Terry laughed to himself anyway as he drove off into the night.

Chapter 2:
The Man's Man

Terry walked into his condo and breathed in a whiff of intense contentedness. Without even turning on the lights he could feel from the tips of his toes, recently nibbled free of any dead skin by a pool of special fish at a spa Terry frequented, to the sharp angles of his jawline and cheekbones just how right everything was inside. New build, concrete construction, every utility, appliance, and building material top of the line. Orderly and minimal, not a breath of clutter to be found. The furnishings were modern cottage in zebra, with a bowl of lemons on every surface large enough to hold one. Every picture on his walls, mostly tasteful nudes, was well hung at the exact right height.

As Terry continued to inhale, however, his finely tuned nose and mind keyed in on two facts. First, his state-of-the-art security system hadn't chimed yet, and second, the slightest hint of an unwelcome umami scent was beginning to reach his olfactory senses.

Terry immediately kicked into high gear, executing a dynamic cartwheel over to an end table and flipping a hidden switch. A panel opened in the wall and a pistol popped out into Terry's waiting hand. At the same time, Terry's high efficiency LED pot lights came on, illuminating and briefly blinding the unkempt man in a baggy overcoat sitting on his couch.

"Who are you, what are you doing here, and why are you wearing your shoes in my living room?" demanded Terry, pointing the gun right at the intruder's chest.

The man on the couch, recovered from the sudden brightness, sat up and looked Terry right in the face. Terry considered himself an expert at reading people, and immediately formed an informed impression. The person in front of him was completely at ease in his home, despite the gun being pointed at him. His unstylish clothing, his lined and slightly jowly visage, and his roughly cut nails indicated a lifetime of hard work and getting his hands dirty. His body, despite its mildly overweight and uncouth exterior, was farm strong and clearly meant business. He was like a footlong sub, carried around in a backpack for too long; the bread might be smooshed, but inside he was all sauce and meatballs. Outward appearances only went so far though. Searching in the man's eyes, Terry instinctively felt a spark of kinship. Those eyes had seen some stuff. Still, Terry had been wrong before, on one very recent and unfortunate occasion in particular, so he remained on high alert.

"You're a hard man to find, Terry. But then again, I'm the best in the business."

Terry didn't like this at all. "No, I'm the best in the business," he replied with some asperity.

The man on the couch chuckled. "Well, you and I are in two different, though not entirely unrelated, fields of business. The name's Dick Richard, I'm a private investigator. And don't get me wrong, your reputation as the best precedes you, though for a spy I'm not sure if that's a good thing. You're at least top two in the continent anyway."

Terry ignored that little dig and gave his guest a smile, revealing straight and perfectly flossed teeth. "Well, I've never heard of you at all. So why don't we cut to the chase, and you tell me why you're in my home with your dirty shoes making a mess that I'm going to have to spend a lot of time vacuuming up? I'm also going to need to freshen the air in here, it smells like garlic."

"Garlic is good for you," Dick grumbled. "Alright. I'm here on behalf of a client. It was his associates you knocked out when they tried to grab you, back at that office building you've now moved on from. I told him that wasn't the way to get you to do business, but he wouldn't listen. He really wanted to see you and it seems like he's into the rough stuff. So now I'm here to try to talk you into meeting him. He's got a job for you."

Terry felt slightly off balance but spoke with what he hoped was cool composure. "Well, I'm not interested. I take jobs at my discretion, that meet my standards. And I do it anonymously. I can't even begin to tell you how disturbed I am that you've somehow tracked me down, which no one has even come close to in the past eight years as far as I know. I'm half temped to just kill you and then go pay a visit with a similar purpose to your boss. The main problem I'm facing right now is that I don't want your blood to get on my things."

"Hey, listen, I'm just doing what I was hired to do," Dick gestured broadly. "I'm a freelancer, like you. I've got no personal interest in your business. Once we're finished talking here, we never have to hear from each other again. But I think you might want to listen, because my boss and I know about your recent incident."

Terry gave a delicate "harrumph," and paused, calculating out where this had all come from and where he thought this might go. "I know the only possible way you could have found me here is that screw-up at the end of my last job. So what does that have to do with what your boss wants? What reason could he give me to take a job for him?"

"Well, maybe not so much a screw-up as a betrayal, am I right?" Terry's face revealed nothing. "Tell you what. I'm going to leave you my card. Why don't you take a look at the data you picked up today, think about what you find, and give me a call?" Dick got up, dusted off what appeared to be Cheeto crumbs from his lap, and walked out the door.

Terry was mystified, stupefied even. Who was this man, and what did he know? How was this related to everything that had happened on that last job? Terry spent the next hour furiously cleaning his apartment with his Dyson cordless vacuum before doing some digging of his own on this Dick Richard. He ferreted away a few nuggets for future use, should the need arrive. Terry then spent the next little while in the bathroom, seeing to his various needs.

Having satisfied those urges, Terry emerged with his flash drive in hand. Loading it up onto his secure mainframe, Terry was stunned. The information itself was nothing special. Typical counter-espionage stuff for a well-paying client. The surprising thing was that over half of it was missing. That seemed impossible. Unless…

Terry grabbed Dick's card off his glass-top tiger-foot coffee table, picked up his phone and dialed. Dick picked up, jovially asking, "So, have you solved the mystery of the missing information?"

"That… that's a terrible name for a mystery," Terry gritted out. "That could describe every mystery ever. How can you… no, shut up. No, talk and keep talking. Only one person could have hacked into that drive, and I want to know what they have to do with this."

"Ah yes," Dick said smugly. "I'm booking you a meeting with my client now. This will be the last you hear from me. But yes, we know what this is about. She's back. She's back and we think she's infiltrated the ranks of my client's business. Going after something big. We need you to find her for us. You've taken on so many jobs. The trans-European man of mystery. So many trysts and romances left behind, stoically moving on to your next hit. But not that one time, not on that last job. The woman you trusted. The woman you thought you were in love with."

Chapter 3:
Balls in My Court

For the second time in as many days, Terry stood facing a comfortably seated man who knew way too much about him. Terry studied the full-figured man seated behind the desk and found that he liked the taste of what he saw. If Dick Richard was dry peanut butter without enough jelly, this man was thick-cut pastrami slathered in mustard. Terry didn't feel at too much of a disadvantage though, because he knew the man facing him liked what he saw too. This was because Terry knew this man, and though they had met in this very building, it was a long time ago and under very different circumstances. Terry had been very surprised to learn where he'd be working on this uninvited job, and especially surprised to learn who the individual who went to such lengths to hire him was, but he had recovered easily enough and had done enough research last night that he knew he didn't let it show.

"How does it feel to be back?" the man at the desk asked him, gesturing around the office. "I believe this is where you spent most of your time when you worked here so long ago. Other than the time you and I spent together... working... in the mail room. Isn't that right, Terrence?"

"You can call me Terrence if you want," said Terry, "But I think you and I both know now that's not my real name, Benjamin."

"Yes, I am aware of that now," said the man at the desk. Benjamin Bogard, CEO of the corporation. A man who had worked his way up from secretary to CEO in just eight years. "You have no idea how often I've thought about you since you left here to seek another opportunity all those years ago. Always as Terrence. Such a disappointment to realize that wasn't your real name. Not a particularly creative alias, was it?"

"Well, it was my first job. I would imagine you know now that I wasn't just another male secretary starting out into the wide world of business alongside you."

"Yes, I'm aware of that too. That only became apparent to me as I moved up the ranks here, gaining access to more and more of our company records. I doubt I would have figured out anything at all if I wasn't so... if you didn't come to mind so often. Not that I was pining. Though as it became more and more apparent to me that you had been here for some purpose other than our clerical duties, it made me wonder what else was a lie. The work we did together, all the... racquetball we played after we would leave for the day?"

An image of a younger Benjamin, drenched with sweat, his form fitting racquetball shorts riding up

slightly as he lunged deeply for a shot, passed
before Terry's eyes. Terry refocused on the
present. "I always enjoyed our games."

Benjamin did not look mollified. "Yes, though
I've come to understand that handball is more your
sport." Benjamin sighed, delicately for a man his
size. "The information you made off with... it set
the company back for years compared to our
competitors. It's part of the reason there was a
vacancy at the CEO level. So, in some ways I
really should thank you. The last time I saw you,
you were headed for a quick steam after we had to
call our game a tie, no one could break the deuce.
But now that I've finally tracked you down, it's
my serve and I've got advantage. And I would love
to take advantage of you... but I mistrust you and I
need your unique skills. So instead, I'm going to
make you a job offer."

"Very well," was all Terry had to say. Calm and
cool on the outside, this conversation was
definitely making him feel some heat.

"I may have meant nothing to you, but I know
of someone who did. Still does, I would imagine.
Dick Richard, with whom you are now acquainted,
told me that the intelligence community, not
having a clue who you are, would probably list you
as nine of the top ten secret agents in the continent.
Well, I think the other entry, and she might just be
number one, is here at my company. She's

somewhere in this building. We have a lot of irons in the fire here. Defense contracts. Private industry. But I've received just the thinnest sliver of a tip that she's after our biggest project, and I only know that because I have someone keeping tabs on our primary rival. I need you to find her. And I think you'll be motivated to do so."

Terry gritted his teeth. So, she was here, was she? Penelope Beanstalk. The woman who had infiltrated the deepest recesses of his usually cavalier heart, turned out to be not who she said she was, stole the cache of data he had worked for weeks to wriggle out of his employer at the time, almost blew his cover, then vanished, crumpling up his feelings like an old brown paper bag that no longer had a sandwich in it. Terry glanced up at Benjamin, realizing he was in the exact same situation he had left Benjamin in. Penelope Beanstalk. God, he hoped that was actually her name. "You probably know that I have an unhappy client from my half-finished last job. And you know that she was somehow behind scooping my haul. So yes, let's keep it professional. That's what's in it for me. Nothing else." Terry said this, but he knew it wasn't true, and he knew that Benjamin knew that too.

"Do this and we're even. I won't blow your cover, and we can go our separate ways again."

So there it all was. Terry tried to look at all the angles. Benjamin knows he has a spy in his midst, and he needs the best spy possible to counter this other spy. Benjamin thinks of Terry, based on their history and what he had put together about him. This other spy also happens to be the one who had bested Terry recently, exposing part of his identity and allowing Benjamin to put Dick Richard on his trail. Terry would be motivated for his own reasons to find her, and to avoid being exposed by Benjamin. The carrot and the stick.

"Fine," Terry said. "And about that past client, if those were your goons that tried, and miserably failed, to jump me back at my last job, I'd like my briefcase back."

"Well, that we can't do." Benjamin lifted Terry's briefcase up from the floor and placed it on the desk. "Consider the paper files in there and the information on them a little leg up for my company to off-set all the setbacks you caused us all those years ago. Besides, it's a nice briefcase and I need a new one. Maybe I'll use it myself." Benjamin tucked the briefcase securely back under the desk.

Chapter 4:
A Job You Can Do With Your Hands

Terry strolled up to the building for his first day of work, looking as tempting as a kielbasa at a support group for recently unwillingly converted vegetarians. He felt like himself again, now that he was pretending to be someone else. Crisp slacks comfortably covering his highly tuned legs, enough room to move but not so much that his finely turned calves weren't obvious. A bespoke collared shirt perfectly fitting over his lean, firm chest and shoulders, tucked in and encircled with a belt that was properly sized for his trim waist. Terry's body was a machine, and he always kept himself well-oiled and lubricated.

Terry was porting a thin mustache and had added a pair of thick glasses to his ensemble. For many men, this would only mildly increase their sexual appeal. For Terry, it somehow accentuated the natural beauty of his face in a way that he knew would make him almost irresistible. Not to mention the Excel skills he planned to employ in his position as executive secretary. Larry, he would be calling himself on this assignment. Larry Broadside.

Despite his exterior veneer of perfection, Terry could feel every muscle in those legs, shoulders and chest tighten as he thought of who he was up against. Penelope Beanstalk. She used his same methods, and he had to admit she was better. Penelope's strength was to confuse, confound. She was always six steps ahead, and also one step right behind you. A master of disguise, and, to Terry's dismay, deceit. Terry used to think he was a master of disguise, but next to her he looked like a master of wearing very ugly, garish clothing. Not the kind of master any man wanted to be. Penelope probably already knew he was coming and would somehow be the first person to greet him when he went through the door.

The person who did meet him, however, was a trim young man. Bordering on short, Terry found something in his compact frame very alluring. "Welcome, Larry," the young man greeted him. "I've been briefed by Benjamin and I'm here to help... orientate you. I'll be your go-to person in all matters that may be important to our mutual boss, Benjamin, if you catch my drift." He winked at Terry conspiratorially.

The young man's open, youthful face inspired trust, and the mildly devious look in his eyes was both charming and enticing. Taken as a whole, however, Terry totally mistrusted the immediately positive feelings this person inspired. He had to ask. "Okay, before we go any further, are you just Penelope in a brilliant disguise?"

The man laughed. "No, unfortunately I am not. My name is Stephan Tellicherry. We'll be working together... very closely on this project of yours."

Stephan spent the morning showing Terry around the building, introducing him to members of the various departments and helping him find key locations, including the lunchroom. Sitting and eating their packed lunches together (arugula salad with grilled halloumi, bee pollen, and raspberry vinaigrette for Terry, and what looked like ambrosia salad for Stephan), Terry decided to trust this appealing fellow. Not everyone was Penelope in disguise, although it was likely she had already infiltrated the building to some extent. Stephan would be a good source of information on who was who in the organization, and who might have been acting strangely recently.

"Pretty healthy lunch," Stephan quipped, pointing his fork over at Terry's meal.

"I'm doing a cleanse following a mild bout of lunchmeat addiction. Now, what do we know about who might have hired… the person we are looking for?" Terry asked.

"Benjamin's suspicion is that Peter Zeria, CEO of a rival company, is behind the data breaches we've been able to detect so far. Peter is a major player in the corporate world and has a specific interest in setting our company back. He would have the means to hire a top-level secret agent to infiltrate us. And… he's a bad dude, from what I know."

Terry had Stephan take him to the mailroom, acting on a hunch that this was where Penelope would first have extended her tendrils into the entrails of the organization. Terry began quickly and efficiently filing away mail, all while keeping an eye out for the telltale signs of Penelope's actions.

Stephan was clearly impressed. "Benjamin said you knew your way around a mailroom, and that you were good with your hands. But this is really something to behold," he said.

"Yes, though it's usually balls that I'm handling," said Terry, thinking back to when Benjamin would have seen him in action. "I used to play handball. I was really good."

"How come you never went pro, made it in the big leagues? With hands like those it sounds like you could have been star!"

"Life got in the way," Terry said darkly. "Speaking of which…" Terry flourished one particular piece of mail, exactly what he'd been looking for. An envelope addressed in such a way that it would keep getting passed around the building, with some unusual heft to it. Opening it up, he slid out a thin electronic device.

"Transmitter device, set to intercept all kinds of signals and to access and download confidential information. She's been here, and that means she's close."

No matter how you sliced it, this job was starting to look like a real roast beef.

Chapter 5:
Taking It in the Ear

Terry stepped out of the shower, pink and steamy from the vigorous scrubbing he had given himself. His torso, so smooth you'd think he had some form of very attractive neck-down alopecia, glistened wetly under the lights of his bedroom as he made his way to his tastefully stocked walk-in closet. On the way he heard the phone ring, and he picked up it, cradling it under one ear. "Hello?" he said.

"Hello Terry," said a husky female voice on the other end of the line. The voice seemed to caress his name in an unspeakably sexual way, the sound of it as hot and tender as a spicy chicken finger. Terry's towel dropped to the floor, leaving him standing entirely naked in the middle of the room.

"Penelope," Terry managed.

"You're looking well," Penelope said. "Nice to see that you're still taking such care of your manscaping."

Terry didn't give her the satisfaction of looking around the room. If she had his apartment bugged, particularly with a video feed, there was nothing to do about it now. Still, the fact that she could see him gave Terry some confidence. His sleek handball player's physique would be the envy of any athletic male, and he knew that thanks to the warm shower he wasn't suffering from any shrinkage at all – more like half-staff really. So he had nothing to be ashamed of.

"Well I think you are sounding very un-well," Terry threw back.

"Now now Terry, be nice. I can tell you like what you're hearing. Plus, I thought we were friends."

"Oh I hear you alright. And I certainly thought you were my friendly, helpful coworker, Penelope Beanstalk. And I also thought we were in love."

"Well, I know you were..."

"Turns out I was wrong about a lot of things. I'm a professional and never should have let my guard down."

"Oh come on Terry!" Penelope laughed. "What was your alias on that job? Thierry? That's barely a disguise at all. You're slipping, Mr. Professional."

That cut Terry deep, leaving him feeling cold. It was a cold cut. Terry was more determined than ever to catch her. It was now very personal. "Perhaps the subtly was lost on you. Either way, I'm going to find you, and I'm going to hand you over to Benjamin, and I really don't want to talk to you anymore right now."

Penelope just laughed again. "Always seven steps behind, dear Terry. You're just getting started but this mystery is actually almost over. I'll be seeing you real soon." And with that, she hung up.

Chapter 6:
Left Unsatisfied

Terry's conversation with Penelope had him on edge. Could he be so far behind the eight-ball that Penelope might be ready to extract with everything she needed already? Terry had spent all night trying to put together a plan for today and had settled on two facts.

Fact one, Benjamin's office building had an expensive proprietary satellite antennae system on the roof, which gave them a major leg up in their line of business. Any rival would probably want to see that dismantled.

Fact two, Terry knew from their time dating that Penelope was a major adrenaline junkie and was fond of jumping off really tall things. Benjamin's building was very tall but had no balconies, with the only exterior access being on the roof.

Putting those two pieces of information together, Terry suspected Penelope's last action before withdrawing would be to blow the array and then make her exit from the building the same way she came in – via the roof (Terry had no proof that she had arrived via the roof, but this detail was still included in his working theory). This seemed more than likely to Terry.

As an initial countermeasure, Terry set up alarms that would trip if anyone tried to access the roof.

Lunch was a tense affair. Stephan and Terry ate in silence, and Terry couldn't relax for long enough to eat the large grapefruit he had packed for dessert. Terry stuffed the grapefruit in his pocket and went back to work before his lunchbreak was complete.

Terry and Stephan were just getting down to some very intense filing when Terry's phone triggered a warning that one of the alarms had been tripped. This was really it then. Day two on the job and already reaching the climax of the story. Terry would find out what Penelope was after and how she'd been hiding herself right now, without any other development leading up to that. Like a bread sandwich, this mystery truly had no middle.

Terry raced up the stairs, quads pumping, with Stephan running close behind. Bursting out onto the roof, Terry quickly assessed the situation. A homemade but very professional looking bomb was strapped to the radio array, and on the edge of the roof, there she was. Flaming locks of auburn hair waving in the wind, wearing a tactical squirrel suit for base-jumping off the building, facemask covering the ivory skin and eyes of emerald green he knew he'd find beneath it. And what was clearly a detonator for the bomb held in her hand.

Reaching into his pocket, Terry pulled out his grapefruit. He was suddenly back on the handball pitch, ball in hand, crowd screaming his name, game on the line. His muscles loosened, feeling totally in control for the first time in days. Terry reached back, gripping his grapefruit tight, then flung his arm forward, unleashing the grapefruit in a perfectly aimed throw. The grapefruit zipped across the open rooftop directly into Penelope's hand, knocking the detonator out of it and off the side of the building.

Unfortunately, the grapefruit also ricocheted off her hand and into her head. Juice squirted out all over her mask. Penelope appeared to be stunned by the hit and began to topple backwards over the side of the roof. Terry raced over to the edge of the building in a mad scramble, lest his archnemesis slash possible soulmate wind up sunny side up on the pavement below. Terry lunged over the side, just barely catching Penelope's arm with his hand. He lay flat on his stomach, just able to hold on to Penelope without being pulled over the edge himself.

He had done it. He had foiled her. And saved her.

Stephan walked into view. "I caught her Stephan!" called Terry. "Help me up and we'll take her to Benjamin."

Stephan just stared at Terry.

"Stephan?" Terry asked, a sinking feeling rising in his stomach.

"That was an impressive display," Stephan said, reaching up and pulling off what was apparently a wig.

"No…" Terry gasped. This could not be happening right now.

"I thought I might get away without blowing my cover," continued Stephan, peeling away further layers of brilliant disguise, revealing a familiar face.

"But you explicitly said that you weren't… Penelope… how…?" managed Terry, while Stephan, now clearly revealed to be Penelope, strapped on a parachute.

"You know how," Penelope smiled. "I'm just that good." Penelope stepped up to the side of the building, preparing to make her departure.

"But… but why?" Terry sputtered, feeling his grip on the dangling person's arm loosening.

"Terry… I wish I could say this was about you." The briefest sad look crossed Penelope's face. She flexed her legs to jump, then turned back to look at him with a grin. "Oh and by the way, I feel like I owe you at least this much. My real name isn't

Penelope. It's Penny." And with that she leaped off the edge, deployed her parachute, and glided away out of Terry's view. Shortly after, the antennae array exploded.

Terry, arm straining mightily, finally managed to pull whoever he was holding onto up onto the ledge. He caught his breath and removed the mask, still sticky from the gushing grapefruit. Behind was the very face he had initially been expecting to see, which momentarily confused him. He was looking at a very realistic mannequin with a very close approximation of Penelope's face and a very accurate wig. Terry unzipped the tactical squirrel suit. Not a mannequin, a sex doll.

Well, he'd be keeping this.

Chapter 7:
Pulling Out

"So Stephan was really Penelope, she was keeping an eye on you the whole time to cover up her own activities, and she completely bamboozled you and got away with our data and damaging our infrastructure. Does that about sum it up?" asked Benjamin.

Terry was once again seated across from Benjamin in his office. "Yeah, I think so," said Terry.

"Curious though. Something else stood out. We've checked our files and she took one other thing. A copy of all our opposition research into Peter Zeria. What do you make of that?"

That did interest Terry, though he couldn't be bothered to respond.

"Well, you know we have you over a barrel. I've been recording all these conversations; I've got evidence and video footage. To say it out loud, I'll be blackmailing you from here on out, and you work for me now on whatever I want. We'll start with sending you to some rival corporations…" Benjamin trailed off as he noticed Terry smiling thinly. "Is something amusing to you?"

"I don't think we'll be doing any of those things," said Terry, touching a remote trigger on his phone. Terry's confiscated briefcase, still tucked away under Benjamin's desk, emitted a powerful electromagnetic pulse, wiping all electronic devices in Benjamin's office, and likely on several other stories of the building. The EMP emitter was the real expense to replacing the briefcases whenever he lost one. Well justified in this case. "I'm sorry Benjamin. It was nice to see you again, but this is the last time we'll cross paths. You really should have let me have my briefcase back," Terry said, getting up and striding calmly out of the room.

Terry stood waiting in the lobby for the elevator, then stepped in when it arrived. His phone started buzzing on the way down. Good signal in this elevator. It was Dick Richard calling. As expected, one last loose end to tie up. Terry answered.

"I've been getting some frantic calls from my old client Benjamin. How'd the rest of the job go?" Dick Richard asked.

"Not quite how I expected," Terry responded.

"Now that you're done there, I figure I should get ahead of things so you don't feel the need to come pay me a visit. I just want you to know that you and I are square," Dick Richard said. "Sure I know some stuff about you, but let's keep that between us professionals. I'm seasoned enough, no need to pepper me with bullets."

"Sounds good to me, Mr. Manwich," Terry responded. "Just in case you get any ideas though, I did some digging on you too and came across some interesting audio content. So as long as this information goes no further, then yes, I'd say we're all square."

Terry hung up and made his way out of the building. It was a nice day outside, blue skies and puffy white clouds. He passed a squished grapefruit and a broken remote on the pavement out front. Time for some new beginnings. Terry had no current commitments, and he hadn't neglected ensuring he'd still get paid from Benjamin's accounts for this job while going about his secretarial duties, lack of results or not. The thick manila folder he'd found in Benjamin's office during some late-night snooping was long incinerated. Time to clean out any online profiles tainted by these last few weeks, and go for some straightforward, high paying jobs with a clean slate. Still… Penelope…no, Penny, was out there. And what was her connection to this Peter Zeria?

He was sure their paths would cross again someday. Their lives seemed like that kind of stringy cheese you'd see in a Middle-Eastern deli, all wrapped together like a ball of cheese yarn. But for now, it was time to get something to eat.

Part 2:

DEAD BATTERY

Prologue:
The Agent

Peter Zeria was a snake of a man. He liked that people said that, he liked hearing that, and he thought of it as a good thing. He was the kind of man who would refer to his arms as pythons, despite the lukewarm reaction women exhibited when he showed off his only moderately impressive biceps. He wasn't exactly sleek and lithe like a snake either, though no one would ever call him pudgy. Not because he wasn't pudgy, he certainly was. It had more to do with the frightening, venomous aura he exuded, or maybe the fact that he had a habit of making people who had offended or displeased him disappear.

Peter's company was the largest producer of batteries for electric cars and vibrators on the continent. No one stayed on top in the highly competitive battery business without a ruthless streak 1.6 kilometers wide, and Peter's was the widest. He cultivated and nurtured this reputation carefully, like a frail and fickle plant of some sort. Peter's business was legitimate, but he of course also had a number of illegitimate buns in the oven at all times. These buns didn't just include his numerous children with his many mistresses; Peter was the proud father of an extensive organized crime family as well.

He had recently had immense success stealing the proprietary information (and delightfully exploding the expensive equipment) of his rival Benjamin Bogard's company, leaving them in the dust. Peter's combination of competitive drive and underhanded villainy had allowed him to amass so much wealth that he had finally branched out into that final frontier of success and power – ownership of a winning professional sports team. Peter's team was the best in the league, maybe on the continent, and would soon have the opportunity to prove it at the most important sporting event in all of Europe, the upcoming continental championships. Additionally, Peter's corporate sponsorship of this tournament, hosted in his team's city, would plaster his name across every surface and screen his ample advertising budget could afford. His power would grow, coiling around his competitors also like a snake.

Peter's phone rang, and he slithered his scaly hands across his desk towards it, darting them out like a cobra to grasp the receiver. His fingers, which maybe he liked to think of as ten very small boa constrictors, strangled the poor phone as he held it up to his face. His tiny, curly moustache, stiffly oiled, brushed against the speaker as he hissed, "this had better be important."

It was important indeed. One of his many carefully placed moles was calling with a very important tip-off, based on some information that had been intercepted. The information caused Peter's mouth to gape open, a string of saliva dangling between his top and bottom teeth, his breath caught in his throat like a piece of carrot he hadn't chewed well enough before trying to swallow it. Intolerably unlike a snake, that kind of experience.

And so was this problem that he was just hearing about. Peter had taken great pains to make certain his precious team would be unbeatable by ensuring they gained some interesting competitive advantages. He couldn't bear the embarrassment that would result from not coming out on top in this tournament. But this news meant his dreams of seeing his precious team hold aloft that trophy could end here, before any games had even been played. No. Nothing could threaten the inevitable victory this tournament would bring him.

Peter's mind quickly calculated the necessary remedy, and his mouth spoke into the phone again. "Yes, this is a problem, and normally I'd have no choice but to shoot the messenger. Lucky for you I believe I have just the person in my employ who can solve this little problem for us." Peter's voice was fat with greasy delight. "She has proven to be… very effective with such matters in the past.

A master of espionage and disguise. A true professional."

Chapter 1:
Big Boules

Terry had balls of steel, and he was currently cupping them in his hands. Surprisingly heavy at two pounds apiece, they felt cool and smooth in his palms as he gently toyed with them. They were each perfectly spherical, and 4.2 inches in diameter. Terry's testicles, on the other hand, which were more like large, plump Medjool dates in shape and size, were firmly pressed against his body, his scrotum having contracted in anticipation of his next move. This was the most intense game of bocce that Terry had ever participated in.

Terry appeared to be at a disadvantage, with both the playing field and his opponent's balls tilted against him. Nevertheless, Terry raised the ball in his right hand up into a throwing position, gauging its heft and the trajectory he'd need to release it at.

Terry had been good at playing with balls his whole life, everyone had always complimented him on this. This would be a difficult shot, but he wouldn't let today be any different. It was all in the fingers, and Terry could have been a hand model. Terry released his ball in a perfect arc, and it clacked against his opponent's ball with a satisfying pétanque. Terry's ball slapped the other ball away, then rolled right up to the boccino, nudging his opponent's other ball aside and moving Terry into the winning position. It was no stretch to say that this was Terry's favorite position. With just one ball each left to throw, Terry was confident of his coming victory. His scrotum relaxed, returning to its normal, attractively dangling shape, without a single hair or wrinkle to be seen.

Having made his move, Terry reached out his arms and stretched them upwards, his perfectly fitting flamingo-patterned shirt riding up just enough to reveal his sculpted abdominal muscles and tight innie bellybutton. It was no coincidence that this was timed exactly with Terry's opponent's throw. Terry's opponent's gaze flicked towards Terry's midriff mid wind-up, and he inhaled a quiet gasp. His ball flew wildly out of his hand and landed far from its mark. Terry enjoyed the thrill of fair athletic competition, but even when he wasn't trying to use his overwhelming sexuality to his advantage, this kind of thing just happened sometimes. Totally intentional today though.

"Looks like I win," Terry said, turning to direct his perfectly shaped and brightly whitened smile at his flustered opponent, while carelessly tossing his remaining ball over his shoulder. Terry's opponent, also his coworker at his most recent gig, wiped the sweat from his brow and quickly closed his slightly agape mouth. "Another come from behind victory. I'll leave you to put the bocce set back in its ballsack. And as per our bet, you must do my filing and yours tomorrow!" His coworker didn't know it, but whether he had won the bet or not, Terry would not be in to work tomorrow. The fact that the documents to be filed away needed clearance only this coworker had, and contained changes and misinformation carefully planted by Terry, didn't really factor into that decision. That was just a final bonus task, icing on the cupcake of this job, and setting up this bocce bet had been the only way to get close enough to someone with access to the right areas. No, the main course of Terry's undercover work at this job was already done, and he wouldn't be in to work ever again, not at this office.

With that business over, Terry turned his attention back to the reason he'd stayed undercover in this job an extra couple of days – the company barbeque picnic going on behind him. It was a beautiful sunny day in the grassy public park. A dozen cooking stations sizzled with juicy meatiness, charcoal flames flicking up to lick the many wieners and sausages lined up on the cast iron grills. Ribs, slathered with sauce, were being finished next to thick beef patties with cheese slices bubbling on top, while brisket and chicken smoked and grew more tender by the minute at the next station. Tables were set with countless side dishes. Pickles, cornbread, coleslaw. Potato salad, pasta salad, salad made with vegetables. Terry had tossed some of those salads himself. He would allow himself to indulge and enjoy the rest of the day. In addition to what he'd be charging his client, he had earned that much.

Just as he was about to engage in the high-stakes decision of which slice of beef he wanted to eat, Terry felt his satellite phone ping, a delightful tingle deep in the pocket of his teasingly short shorts, indicating that he had a message waiting for him. He discreetly stepped aside from the food line and checked his phone. What he saw was very interesting indeed. A secure message from a high-ranking official of the European Union to one of his many aliases. They only resorted to off-the-books contractors like himself for the most important missions.

Terry got back in line and filled a plate with an appropriate balance of meats and sides. His recovery from his lunchmeat addiction over a year ago was an ongoing struggle, one he faced every day. He was proud of how he had made it through those times and that he was now able to enjoy the carnivorous delights of meat alongside other food too. He glanced around at the other picnic activities. Badminton, disc golf, croquet. Signs of a volleyball net going up. His phone buzzed again, that same little thrill letting him know that further details on this new job would be waiting for him. He'd have liked to stay longer, but he'd have to take his plate of food and eat it on the go. It looked like it was time for Terry to go back undercover on another job.

Chapter 2:
A Pizza the Action

The official that had covertly contracted Terry turned out to be the Minister of Sport. Terry had to laugh. This same man had once pinned a medal on Terry's chest as the Best and the Fairest at the U21 continental championships back during Terry's university days, when he also represented his country on the handball national team. Terry knew that this same man had personally put many resources toward hunting Terry down when he'd made himself vanish to take up his life of clandestine espionage work, trying to find out just what had happened to the star player that the whole country had come to admire and depend on, and where he'd disappeared to. That Minster was closer than ever to finding him. He would have no idea who he was really communicating with of course, it was just a coincidence. But Terry also felt a small stab of, if not guilt, then regret, knowing the team had never been the same since.

An EU Minister of Sport hiring an agent of Terry's caliber could only be related to the most important of sports, and that was indeed the case. The governing body of the upcoming European Baseball Championship had quietly contacted the

Minister because of their concerns around a potential doping scandal at the tournament. The host team, highly favored to win it all, had taken a statistically unlikely spike in their performance over the past few months, and their apparent gains in the gym appeared equally unlikely. New drug testing protocols had been implemented right away, which included testing the entire host team. However, no player's urine had come back positive yet. The samples were actually suspiciously clean. Complicating matters was the fact that the team's owner, Peter Zeria of the Zeria electric car and vibrator battery manufacturing group, was also the tournament's corporate sponsor. The Zeria corporation had even erected a brand-new stadium, complete with enormous company logo, just for this tournament. It was clearly a delicate situation. Terry's job was to uncover what he could about the possible scandal, and to prevent the national outrage that would occur if it was discovered that a team had been allowed to win by cheating this way.

Terry liked ball sports and hated cheating, so this job would be a real pleasure for him. There was also one other important reason why Terry was particularly interested and pleased to have received this job, one that had nothing to do with the Minister's tasks. It was the name Peter Zeria.

Terry had encountered the work of Peter Zeria's company before in that ill-fated adventure last year. Terry had been contracted for a job against his will thanks to the industrious sleuthing of one Dick Richard. He had been brought into his old friend (and Zeria's rival) Benjamin Bogard's company to root out a secret agent of Zeria's, who had been planted there to cause trouble. There was more backstory to it than that, but it had all gone sideways, largely because the secret agent in question was Penny.

Over the course of their multiple encounters Penny had stolen Terry's heart, betrayed him, outsmarted him and betrayed him again, and disappeared. That job was the last time Terry had seen that woman, and all he had to go on was that she had some mysterious connection to and was working for this Peter Zeria. Thinking of her caused many feelings to erupt in Terry's stomach. Desire. Frustration. Bewilderment. Hunger. Desire.

In the year since that last encounter, Terry had been looking over his shoulder a little bit the whole time, expecting to find Penny everywhere. Penny had never turned up so far, but he couldn't believe that a job related to Peter Zeria wouldn't see Penny involved somehow. He wasn't sure how, but this was no coincidence. Terry still wasn't sure what this Peter had on Penny that resulted in her working for him, or what their connection really was. She should be able to be a free agent, like him. Did Peter have some sort of hold on her? Did she need Terry's help? Maybe this job would be a way to find out, if he could find her. Penny was, after all, a master of disguise.

Terry had done his research. Peter Zeria was clearly a mobster, that much was plain to see. Smuggling, racketeering, having people whacked, the whole thing. He was involved in a lot more than his public face would indicate, but his company was legitimately a major player in the world of technology, and consequently corporate espionage. And the Zeria company specialized in batteries. Batteries. Ba-Terrys. That couldn't be a coincidence either. Terry knew this was about him, somehow.

Terry studied his computer screen, playing a video of Peter cutting the ribbon on his new ballpark. This was not an impressive looking man. He was so doughy Terry could practically see the flour puffing off of him when he moved. His sense of style was cheesy, and Terry was somehow sure Peter's nipples would look like two big slices of pepperoni. Yet he also steamed with a clear sense of danger, straight out of the oven. Like a pizza where the toppings were put on right after the sauce instead of last, you never knew what might be hiding under the surface.

Well, there was only one thing a pizza was afraid of, and that was a man with an appetite, and Terry was nothing if not a man of appetites. It was time to blow on that pizza so it didn't burn his tongue, and dig in.

Chapter 3:
Back on Top

A few days later, Terry was back on the job, and for the first time in a year was finally feeling back on top. It wasn't often that the chapter name appeared in the chapter, much less so in the first sentence, but this new role had Terry feeling great about himself and feeling very much back on top indeed. Coming off a recent string of consecutive successful jobs, he had built himself back up. The hard work had enriched him financially and spiritually, satisfied him professionally, and had now more than made up for the onerous boners from his misadventures last year. And now this latest job, one of his highest profile jobs yet.

Terry had approached this new job using his usual methods. He had dazzled everyone in his interview and secured employment for himself as the travelling secretary to the baseball team he was to investigate. This kept his profile low but gave him high level access to all areas of the team facility, and allowed him to travel with the team and to observe the players closely. Very closely. He was using another impenetrable moniker in this role, Gary Boardside.

Terry filled his days keeping his eyes open while going about his secretarial work. Eyes open in the boardroom while team executives held conferences and looked at possible matchups. Eyes open on the field, as the players practiced their batting and fielding. Eyes open in the changing room and the gym, of course.

Performing his secretarial duties, Terry fetched various complex coffee orders, saw to the timely filing of reports, and attended meetings where he took minutes. Terry loved taking minutes. He would take hours, if he were allowed to. No time for that today though, Terry would have to make do with taking more minutes during his leisure time.

The first thing Terry had noticed in his time around the team was that almost all the players were huge. He had come in thinking he'd be digging around to determine which one of the players might be juicing, but based on the extreme musculature of the men around him, it wasn't just one player. Was this team abusing performance enhancing drugs? Almost certainly, mystery solved. In this scandal, nearly every player was as embroiled as cheese and bacon on toast. What Terry couldn't figure out yet was how they were getting away with it, or who was helping them to do so.

There were high expectations for the team this year, particularly thanks to the expenses that had gone into hosting the championship tournament. Terry read through every piece of information he could get on the players. This team was a true five-alarm chili of batting for power, batting for average, throwing, running the bases, and fielding. Scouting reports indicated that almost every member of the team had proactively had Tommy John surgery, even the position players, making them a nearly unstoppable force on the field. There would be no elbow tenderness on this team, no matter what they did with their arms. That wasn't illegal, though it was ethically and medically questionable.

Terry, ostensibly doing some paperwork in the changing room where the players were winding down from their practice, looked around at the members of this team. The starting pitchers were sitting in ice baths, the bullpen pitchers were having a steam. The batters were all using grip strengthening tools, that kind that you squeeze with your hand. This was so they could hold really tightly on to the shaft of their bats, which was an important skill in baseball. It probably helped them to grip their balls tightly too. Terry watched for a few moments, their enormous forearms flexing and growing more defined with each rep.

Terry suddenly felt that telltale tingle on the back of his neck, like he was also being watched. Terry had learned to trust this instinct, and he calmed himself to ensure he didn't show any reaction. He'd been expecting this. It seemed likely that almost each and every one of these players was actually Penny in disguise, maybe with a muscle suit. Well, probably just one of them, but he wouldn't put it past Penny to be in more than one place at a time. She was that good, and it was only logical that she was somewhere close. He'd been careful to observe the players without their clothes on, of course, but hadn't been able to see any signs of which of them might not be who they said they were.

Terry reflected that he had said "almost" and "nearly" when referring to the generally juiced-up group of players on this team. The one exception was their captain, third baseman Jay McGriff. Jay was the most feared batter in the whole league, a switch hitter with equal skill on both sides of the plate. He was so skilled Terry wished he would bat for both teams, just to be able to see him in action that much more often. Jay was an excellent defender and could launch a rocket when throwing from third to first, every motion silky smooth. He was also the only player Terry would believe if he were to deny using steroids.

Terry busied himself with some papers and clipboards while he studied Jay. Jay had closely buzzed light brown hair, and a few hours of stubble growth on his cheeks. Tall and handsome, he even changed out of his baseball uniform gracefully. Unlike his teammates, his strength and size looked natural, the ideal corn-fed European of American descent farm boy baseball physique. Yes, Terry could easily picture Jay on a farm, wearing nothing but a pair of overalls, his bare, broad shoulders pinked from the sun, sweat streaming down his arms as he bailed hay with a pitchfork. Some hay would stick to his forehead as he wiped his brow, and Terry would be there to gently reach over and pick it off for him…

Jay's agent, Pepper O'Neil, entered the room. She was a serious and efficient woman. When Terry had heard she was an agent, he had immediately gone on high alert, until he had realized she was a sports agent, the contracts and business kind of agent, not a secret agent. Totally different. She was very dedicated to her client, and was here today working on a sponsorship deal between Jay and the Zeria corporation. Terry wasn't sure which of their products he would be advertising. "They're ready for you," she called to Jay. "You'll just need to stop by the team physician office to complete their urine testing requirements first."

The whole team would be undergoing another round of urine tests today and would each have to provide a repeat sample. The chain of custody of these pee containers would be a key clue for Terry's work. Jay stood up and dropped his sweaty jock strap into the laundry bin, heading for the door. "Pee right back!" Jay announced to the room before strolling out. He disappeared around the corner, following Pepper down the hall.

This was an important moment. Terry needed to see what was happening with these urine tests. He quietly slipped out of the room, glancing around discretely to make sure he wasn't observed as he tried to catch up with Jay and tail him on the way to the doctor's office.

Terry snuck down the hallway, as light and careful on his feet as a deer. "I'll catch up with you," he heard Pepper say, and he heard her footsteps fading away in another direction. Terry continued down the hall, sure he was about to catch up to Jay as he rounded the next corner in the hallway. At just that moment Terry heard a sudden crash, and he dashed toward the source of the noise.

There on the ground was Jay, not moving or breathing, lying in a pool of baseball bats and his own blood. Terry had seen his share of dead bodies, and the team's top batter was clearly dead. This wasn't just an investigation into a steroid

scandal anymore. It was now a murder
investigation.

Chapter 4:
Assault and Battery

Jay, so recently alive and beautiful, was sprawled out on the ground among various pieces of baseball equipment, which had apparently been scattered across the floor from their nearby tipped-over storage bin. Jay's pants were unzipped and his penis was out, his urine sample cup on the ground next to his outstretched hand. His body was covered in bruises and contusions in addition to the many gashes on his head that contributed to the growing quantity of blood staining the carpet, and his foot was dangling at a funny angle.

"He's been murdered!" cried Pepper, rushing into the hallway, the rest of the team following close behind her. "It looks like someone beat him with those baseball bats! Who could have done this?"

Terry studied the scene, careful not to touch anything. "Why was his penis already out…?" Terry wondered aloud. He idly pondered how long it would take for rigor mortis to set in. It was all too horrible. Terry took a crisply folded handkerchief out of his pocket and held it in front of his nose to ward off any smells Jay's body might start to make.

Murdered on the way to providing a urine sample, there was no way this wasn't related to the cover-up. But it didn't make any sense. There was no way Jay was using steroids. On top of the other evidence, one look at Jay's generously sized testicles had confirmed that. There had to be something else going on here.

The whole hallway was bubbling over with concerned teammates and staff. Someone had the good sense to run for the team doctor, who immediately took charge of the scene and checked Jay's pulse. "This baseball man is dead," he announced. Pepper O'Neil, who had seemed so distraught, stood to the side of the hallway with a thoughtful look on her face.

Building security, with annoying efficiency, started to clear everyone away, and the police also arrived in an irritatingly timely manner. Terry was glad that he wasn't in one of those situations where he was accused of the murder for being in the wrong place at the wrong time, due to the compromising situation he could have found himself in just now. It was certainly a relief to avoid that particular cliché. Terry hadn't had the opportunity to examine Jay's whole body though, or to look for other clues. He'd have to find another way to do so.

Terry spent the rest of the day on autopilot, going about his secretarial duties while mulling over the events of the morning. The loss of Jay McGriff at third base and at the top of the batting order meant there would need to be a major reorganization of the roster. Curiously, no one floated the idea of a trade. They'd make do with promoting another player off the bench, though of course no one individual player could replace their leadoff man.

Finally, Terry overheard something he could use, which was that Jay's body would be kept onsite in the stadium kitchen's walk-in freezer while the police investigation continued. Unsanitary as it sounded, that would be Terry's opportunity.

His duties for the day concluded, Terry stealthily made his way down to the kitchen. Most of the kitchen space was dedicated to making protein shakes, with multiple blenders set up on the various counters. The walk-in freezer, which mostly contained frozen berries and bananas, was at the back of the room. Terry walked over and began to open the freezer door, when he suddenly heard movement from within the freezer, along with the distinct crinkly zipping sound of the sterile plastic sleeve of a piece of medical equipment being opened. Someone had beaten him here.

Terry inched the door open, but it gave a loud and obvious squeak. The sounds from within the freezer immediately stopped. Terry braced himself against the door, preparing to spring it open and to say a cool one-liner, probably something about freezing. Unfortunately, a small explosive device bounced out through the small gap in the door, landing at his feet and immediately giving off a large plume of smoke. Terry was disoriented, bent over coughing, and through his stinging and watering eyes was only able to make out the shape of a person shoving the door open and running past him out of the kitchen. By the time the smoke cleared and Terry was able to check the hallway, whoever that had been was long gone.

Terry went back into the freezer to see what he could find. Jay's body was in there on a simple metal gurney, and the body bag he had been stored in was unzipped down past his waist. Terry found two curious items on the floor. One was an empty urine sample container, and the other was a urinary catheter, recently opened from its packaging but clearly unused. This mystery was deepening into a very deep dish indeed. Someone had tried to steal Jay's urine right out of his dead bladder. Terry looked around for anything else he could use, but there was no documentation or autopsy report to be found, at least not stored in here.

Somewhat dejected with his progress, Terry pocketed the evidence, covered his tracks, and exited the building to the staff parking lot. A small group of reporters were still hanging around, hoping to pluck out any new details on the events of the day. A particularly forward reporter, also particularly attractive, to Terry's eyes, pushed forward and held her microphone in front of his face.

"Annie Kometz, reporter for the news! Any comments you can share with us about what happened today? What do you think this is about?"

Terry knew he was looking good today. He'd trimmed his moustache just right and picked out his suspenders specifically to accentuate how he'd been working out his chest a bit more these days. He was also very hungry and wanted someone else to pay for his food, so he figured he'd give it a shot.

"If you want, I can give you… exclusive access to some inside knowledge. If you'd like to buy me dinner, that is," Terry said, taking advantage of the opportunity provided to him.

The reporter, Annie, smiled knowingly. She wrote something on a piece of paper and told Terry to meet her in twenty-five minutes. The piece of paper turned out to have an address on it, and following it led Terry to the entrance to a classy seafood restaurant. The address was in easy walking distance from the ballpark, so Terry had made his way over by foot. Annie arrived a few minutes after him, and they both ordered beer battered fish and chips, with lemonade to drink.

Annie sat across from Terry at a high table by the window. As they sat waiting for their food and making small talk, the romantic tension began to steadily increase. When the fish and chips were brought to the table, perfectly crispy and not too oily, the erotic environment of course grew exponentially. They ate quickly, and in silence, their eyes speaking volumes. Terry was not at all surprised when Annie suggested he come over to her place, which was conveniently across the street in a low-rise luxury condo building. It appeared that this evening was becoming very interesting indeed.

The elevator ride to the top floor, which was only the fourth floor, took forever, and the sexual energy at that point felt like it would make the elevator shaft explode. They finally made it into Annie's apartment, and it was then abundantly clear; it was time for a sex scene.

Chapter 5:
Rounding the Bases

It had been a long time since Terry had had a sex scene. It wasn't that he was going through a dry spell or anything. It had just been a while. Terry was a skillful and considerate lover, with excellent control over himself and an innate sense of what others needed. It also clearly wasn't from lack of opportunities that he hadn't made any recent connections. He had just become… very selective over the past year and a bit.

Today felt differently though. He barely had time to look around the sparsely furnished apartment he found himself in before being pulled into the bedroom, also decorated in a fairly nondescript way.

Terry swiftly removed his clothing, revealing his smooth and ripped muscles. The veins on his forearms popped out, his forearm muscles, which he exercised very often, looking very thick and defined. He used the hands on the ends of those forearms to fold each item of clothing neatly, ensuring that they would not become wrinkled on the ground.

Terry was pleased to see that Annie had also taken off her clothes, though she had left her clothes in a messy pile on the floor. Terry's penis, which had been progressively engorging, softened more than a little at seeing that. Annie stepped over the pile of clothes and strode right up to Terry. She reached up and twizzled Terry's nipples. That seemed to more than make up for the laundry issue, with his penis standing up tall and proudly, though not imperiously. Terry's recently manicured toes curled in anticipation. A little bit of messiness and clutter could be forgiven in times like this.

After that, things got very nasty, but Terry didn't feel like describing them any further. It was sort of embarrassing to even narrate the previous paragraph. Regardless, the action got very packed, and needless to say it was a very long sex scene, even if that isn't necessarily translated here on the page.

After a vigorous and satisfying bout of activity, Terry and Annie lay back on the bed; Annie exhausted, Terry not really tired, thanks to his high level of fitness and stamina, but feeling like he'd had a nice workout.

Terry, who hadn't been hydrating himself extremely well today but also hadn't had an opportunity to pee in ages, got up from the bed and headed into the bathroom. He had really just had that lemonade since Jay's murder earlier in the day. The toilet, strangely, looked totally dry and didn't seem to have a drain. Some new model,

perhaps. Terry had just finished emptying his
large, high-capacity bladder when he felt a blow
on the back of his head. Stars burst before his eyes,
he lost his balance, and he hit the ground,
immediately blacking out.

Chapter 6:
Duodenouement

Terry came to and took stock of himself. What had happened? Had Annie knocked him out? That didn't really make sense. How had she snuck up on him anyway? That would take no small measure of skill. He looked at the clock on the wall of the bathroom. Only a few minutes had passed. Terry glanced in the toilet and was shocked to find that his pee was gone. He hadn't flushed, he would have remembered that. What was going on here? He stumbled over to the window, and saw Annie running across the parking lot, with what looked like a zip-loc bag of liquid-filled cylinders gripped in her hand. Terry put the available pieces together. Annie had stolen his urine and put it into several small containers. But why?

Terry started racing down the stairs, then resorted to just sliding down the railings on his bum, because that was much faster. He charged through the exit door just in time to see Annie hop in her car, a big ugly pick-up truck, and drive away. A car chase scene was about to ensue.

Terry raced over to where he had parked his car in the nearby stadium's staff parking lot, his bare feet slapping the ground loudly as he ran. It was the middle of the night and silent, with barely another car to be seen. Terry admired his car as he approached it, and realized he was fully erect, in fact much more erect than he had been at any point during his recent sexual encounter with Annie. This wasn't embarrassing for Terry though; it was actually the normal and expected reaction for anyone who saw a vehicle like Terry's – an absolute babe magnet of a Nissan Cube. Noticing his erection also alerted Terry to the fact that he was wearing nothing but the pair of seamless underwear he had slipped into on the way to the bathroom after getting out of bed. Not really a problem, just not what he'd usually wear during a car chase.

Terry leapt into the driver's seat of his car and swallowed in anticipation before activating the push-button start, his palms sweating lightly. His car started with barely a sound, the electric motor not purring in the slightest. His car wouldn't make any perceptible noise at all, even at top speed.

Terry was still a bit bleary from being hit in the head. Fortunately, Terry's vehicle was automatic, so he didn't need to worry about shifting gears or anything silly like that. This was much better for a chase scene, because he could just focus on driving, and was also much more fuel efficient and environmentally friendly.

Terry took a few moments to appreciate the spacious, boxy interior of his Nissan Cube. He loved its squared off angles and ample storage space. No other cube-shaped car out there even came close. She would not fail him tonight. Terry put the car in reverse, pulled out, and pushed the pedal to the metal.

Terry quickly caught sight of Annie's vehicle and moved to overtake her. Driving at high speeds was very dangerous; Terry needed to stop Annie before either of them had an accident or before someone got hurt. He didn't have a grapefruit or any other handball-like fruit to help him this time. He'd have to go with his guts.

Terry pulled up behind Annie, but to his surprise she seemed to be just making a loop and heading back to where they'd started. Terry's guts decided to tell him to just follow Annie, which to his continued surprise resulted in them pulling up in front of the staff entrance to the new Zeria-branded baseball stadium where they had met earlier in the day. Annie got out of her vehicle and was heading for the doors. Though this had been a pretty short and simple car chase scene, Terry at least did a cool hand-break maneuver as he pulled to a stop, swerving in front of Annie and blocking her path.

"Hold it right there, Annie! I don't know what you're doing with all those urine containers full of my pee, but you'll never get away with it!" Terry hopped out of his car and stood facing her.

Annie was clearly shocked to see him standing in her way. "I'm afraid I can't let you stop me. I can't allow my employer's team to lose this tournament, and that starts with not letting the team get caught for steroid use. You'll just have to get out of my way."

"Wait, you aren't a reporter, and you work for the Zeria company?"

"Annie Kometz the reporter was just another brilliant disguise. I've been here this whole time, planning to outsmart anyone who tried to catch us in the act. You see, we heard the league would be drug testing our players. But as long as we had Jay McGriff, and me here to make use of him, we knew we were in the clear. You've probably deduced that this whole operation wasn't about preventing just one of our players from testing positive. The whole team would have been positive, and they were all in on it, willing participants. Everyone but Jay. Jay was the only player on the team who didn't use steroids and who didn't know about our little conspiracy. We needed his pee to get the rest of the team to pass the drug tests. My job was to swap their samples out for Jay's. He never had any idea why we always made him give such enormous pee samples. That's also why I was posing as Pepper O'Neil, Jay's agent, to stay close to Jay and so I could flush out whoever the sports commissioner would inevitably send after us to investigate."

Terry definitely hadn't picked up on that last part. He had sort of forgotten about Pepper. She must have changed her costumes very quickly. "But what about the murder? If Jay was so important to your plans, why did you have him killed? Was he going to turn on you?"

Annie laughed. "What murder? It may not have been obvious to you, but it was clear to me that Jay simply ruptured his Achilles tendon on the way to the bathroom and fell into that pile of baseball bats. Poor Jay. It's a very common baseball injury, though he was unlucky that this time it was fatal."

Terry was really thrown for a loop here and tried to think this through. The big reveal in this mystery was not quite what he had expected. Was this non-murder reveal just a throwaway? No, it was a necessary cover-up and essential part of the story. "So all that talk of murder was just a beer battered red herring, and it was you who was going to steal his urine from the kitchen freezer. When the accident happened you needed it to look like a murder so his body wouldn't be taken off site right away, and so you could still have access to it and its precious pee one last time. You, as Pepper, were acting on the fly. But what about what was happening earlier, at the time of the murder? I mean, not murder, but when Jay was killed by those bats. Why was his penis out when he died?"

"That was just Jay showing his typical hustle, getting ready to provide his sample. He never did anything halfway. That's why he was so good at baseball. A huge loss."

That part, at least, did make sense to Terry. "So, where do we go from here?"

"Well, now that Jay is gone, we need another athletic European male's pee. That's where you come in. You and your clean, untainted pee, which we're going to swap out for everyone else's samples. I'm going to deliver this pee to the lab, our team will pass, and we'll be allowed to get away with it and win this tournament without any silly questions about why our players are so jacked."

"I don't think so," said Terry, getting ready to take action.

"Of course, we'll have to frame you as some sort of spy from the other teams, to deflect suspicions away from us. That'll be a lot easier if you die."

Annie whipped out a gun, quickly aiming it at Terry. Terry swiftly executed a standing backflip, landing directly behind his car. Annie fired off a tight cluster of bullets, one of them glancing off the gleaming side panel of his Nissan Cube. The bullet ricocheted off the indestructible car and deflected directly back at Annie, hitting her in a non-lethal spot and dropping her to the ground.

Terry carefully walked over to her, kicking away her gun. This had been a most interesting evening, but now it was over and he had apprehended the villain. This job had been an outright victory, no half measures this time. Now all that was left was the second big reveal. It was time to unmask Annie Pepper and unveil who she truly was, which was clearly Penny.

Terry pulled at Annie's hair, then her face. Neither would come off. "Hmm," he said to himself, and he felt around at her neck to see where the mask attached.

"Ow, what are you doing?" yelled Annie. "I'm not wearing a mask."

Annie wasn't Penny. Now that he took the time to really assess the situation, that seemed very clear to him. To Terry's complete shock, it appeared that Penny was not part of this mystery at all. He was plain wrong about Penny being there. This was just some other person.

"I know who you think you're looking for. Did you think she was the only qualified female secret agent taking jobs for the Zeria company?" Annie laughed, which turned into a cough. "I'm good, but not that good. Penny would never be caught by the likes of you."

This case truly had more twists than a whole case of Pepsi Twist. Terry handcuffed Annie and left a long note explaining the situation to the police, who he then called. Hearing sirens in the distance, Terry turned to leave, a cloud dampening his thoughts. It was time to drive off into the night and think this over.

Chapter 7:
A Penny For Your Thoughts

Terry was back in his home, pouring himself a tall kombucha out of the large glass jar he brewed it in. He fondly patted his scoby on the head before putting the jar back in the cupboard next to the many boxes of tea and other scoby foods.

He sat down in his most comfortable chair to relax. He had thoroughly showered, exfoliating his body and tidying up all of his personal grooming. He put on his cozy terrycloth robe and slipped his long feet into his large, fuzzy, and practical slippers. The news was just playing the story now. Peter Zeria had declined comment, but his team was already being disqualified from the tournament. The players were all suspended and could kiss their season goodbye. This was a huge embarrassment for the CEO and his organization, and would result in major losses for the company, even if Zeria himself would escape without direct implication.

Terry knew he'd now be on Peter's radar, so he had taken pains to erase all signs of his involvement in this case. He'd covered his tracks well, but he'd have a new enemy. One that could find him if he could connect him to Penny, and somehow make her give up what she knew about him. Ah well. At least ole Pete had egg on his face, and the sanctity of baseball was once again preserved, for now.

Other than not properly identifying who the villain was and sort of falling into the solution at the end, Terry had gotten everything right this time. He'd accomplished everything that had been asked of him, and the Minister of Sport was thrilled with the results. So why didn't he feel happy about that?

Realizing he wasn't happy made Terry shed some manly tears. Thinking about it, Terry realized that the events of the previous year had had a more profound and damaging impact on him than he had wanted to admit to himself. The specter of Penny hanging over him, ready to break his heart and damage his professional reputation, had clearly been an intense stress on his mind. His confidence was shaken. She had really gotten to him.

If this investigation had taught Terry one thing, it was that he needed to get over his paranoia of Penny being everywhere, and everything being about Penny. It was time to pivot, both in action and thought. Maybe he and Penny weren't like a ball of cheese yarn, like he used to think. Maybe they were like a bowl of spaghetti, which looked like it could be one big, long noodle but was actually many noodles. And maybe with some parmesan cheese on top, and Terry was the…

Terry's phone buzzed, and he answered it. The voice on the other end of the line was like leftover bread crusts. "Terry, it's Dick Richard. We need to talk. I think you'll be interested, it's about your old flame, Penny."

Never mind all that then. Learning lessons about things could wait for some other time.

Part 3

SIX INCHES

Prologue:
Nine Years Ago

A generic looking man stood on his toes to get a better look. He felt like he was in heaven; fourteen sweaty young men were performing for him, breathing heavily and grunting with effort. They were all strong, athletic, and skilled. And the best part was, he was being paid to be here. Damn, he loved being a professional sports journalist, and he loved the sport of team handball, no matter who was playing it.

The men on the court were the best of the best. This was the collegiate national championships, one of the most watched sporting events of the year. Despite the wealth of talent before him, one player in particular stood out. A sterling defender, a stalwart teammate, a crisp passer, and most of all a deadly scorer, there was something about young Terry O'Broadside that drew the eye. Twenty-two years old, in his final year of eligibility for college handball, he was likely to be the first overall pick in the upcoming professional draft. Though the style for players had shifted towards wearing longer, baggier shorts, Terry still wore the much more functional and sensible short shorts, showing a length of powerful quadriceps on each leg that left very little to the imagination. Terry's thighs pumped up and down, flexing and releasing as he effortlessly loped down the playing area on defense, blocking a pass from an opponent and causing the ball to land in the hands of one of his teammates. "Damn good handball player," the journalist said to himself, writing down notes for his article. "And HOT!"

Terry sprinted down the court, weaving through the defenders. He received a pass from his teammate with a graceful hop, evading the many grasping hands around him, landed, and pivoted toward the goal. Terry easily palmed the round, firm, almost juicy sphere in his hand. The journalist felt his heart pounding, feeling the same rush of adrenaline Terry must be feeling, feeling like his heart and the hearts of the entire crowd were beating in sync with Terry's. Terry gave the ball a good squeeze with his wide hands, his clever fingers running over the grippy material. Sweat attractively moistened his forehead, his flowing hair damp around his headband. Terry's moustache, just a fine sprinkling of soft hairs, absorbed the sweat from his upper lip. Everyone knew this was the moment. It was all on the line.

Thanks to his many years of training as a reporter and his knowledge and experience covering the game, the journalist could easily follow even the smallest developments in play on the court before him. He could feel the pressure on

Terry and his teammates, thought to be the favorites, who were deadlocked in a tie with the scrappy underdogs they faced. And with so little time left on the clock, the next goal would assuredly go down as the game winner.

The journalist felt like he was out there himself, though he had never had an ounce of sporting ability. He could see that over to Terry's left, sneaking in from behind, was Terry's most trusted friend and teammate, Walter, a left-handed shot, who quickly called for the ball. Walter was the assistant captain to team captain Terry, and the second-best player out there. Terry could make that pass, and there would be an opening for Walter to take shot on net. With the defenders swarming Terry it would be a much cleaner look for the taller, lankier player. It was the safest and most high percentage play. The journalist glanced up at the game clock, which was quickly ticking down toward zero. In front of Terry, who stood surveying the court around him, was a nearly impossible shot, with multiple opponents blocking the view of the net in front of him, aware of the threat Terry posed.

Walter called for the ball again, catching just the slightest bit of the goalie's attention. Terry glanced one last time over at Walter, then took a deep breath. The journalist could almost read Terry's mind. They had to win. Who else but Terry could guarantee that? That look was in his eyes; he had seen the goalie's brief moment of distraction. Terry didn't pass. He focused on that one tiny sliver of possibility of scoring and rifled off the impossible shot.

It went in of course. They had won. As the crowd surged to their feet with joy, Terry and Walter turned and looked at each other, elated. They took a step toward each other in celebration, but at that moment the rest of the team came off the bench and swarmed Terry, picking him up and carrying him in the other direction from Walter. Terry had time to look back and see Walter's smile of victory recede into familiar resignation. As Terry's name was chanted aloud for all to hear, that look of resignation drifted, just briefly, into one of an angry, deep jealousy.

The article the journalist published the next morning covering the game was maybe excessively focused on one player, the hero of the day. But who could argue with the results? And who would go back and suggest that Terry do anything other than shoot in that moment?

It was a decision Terry had made many times and in many games. That kind of decision making would go on, in part, to create the success he found in his professional life, working alone. But it was one question Terry often asked himself when looking back at his time playing team sports, and the fallout from that final game that caused him to stop playing forever. Why did he never pass?

Chapter 1:
The Meat-Up

Back in the present, Terry, now 31 years old but looking better than ever, had recently received an intriguing phone call from an old… well, acquaintance was maybe the nicest way to put it. The call had been from Dick Richard, the private eye who had pierced Terry's careful veil of secrecy. A man that Terry found, on the surface, to be gross and yucky, though maybe also a little bit interesting and intimidating, if he was being honest with himself. And now Terry was going to see him.

Terry didn't want to meet with him. He didn't want to be pitted against Dick Richard in a race to solve some mystery or something, wherever this was going, but he couldn't turn down the meeting. The circumstances of their previous encounter, in which Dick Richard had managed to track him down to his home using just the slimmest of clues as a starting point, meant he had to assume that Dick Richard had also been able to pry open all of Terry's most embarrassing secrets. And if Dick was suggesting they meet in person, it meant Dick was prepared to use those secrets as a shield, to protect himself if necessary. Terry wasn't unprepared or anything. He had made sure to pull on his own ample resources and brush up on his research into all of Dick's hidden secrets as well, so Terry at least felt like he was entering the situation with a sword in hand.

Terry walked up to the entrance to the building that housed Dick's office. The façade was as crumbly and chewed up looking as a tough old biscuit, and the glass on the front door was as foggy as an Earl Grey latte. Terry pushed the intercom button.

There was another reason Terry couldn't turn down this meeting. Penny. The reason Dick Richard had called in the first place was to tell Terry he had information on her, and Terry couldn't pass that up. Penny was why he was here. Terry hadn't seen her since the last time he had seen her, and that had not gone well. So here he was.

Terry zoned out while the intercom rang and rang, picturing all his previous encounters with Penny. Finally, the ringing stopped as someone picked up. Startled, Terry's heart sprang up in his chest. He rushed to straighten his already straight hair, images of Penny occupying all of Terry's brain space. He could already hear the musical lilt of her speaking his name. He leaned in toward the intercom.

"Terry," said a familiar voice. Terry's heart dropped right back down, maybe to a few inches below where it normally sat. Not the voice he'd been thinking of, but a scratchy, deep voice that tickled unpleasantly to listen to. Of course it wasn't her, wasn't Penny. Terry knew that. He was here to meet Dick Richard, had been expecting Dick Richard. But Terry was here to talk to him about Penny. And Terry was just muddled, that was all, letting his imaginings of himself and Penny flood his mind. He had just been on the cusp of getting over Penny, and now she was back in his life once again. How many more times was his internal narrative going to say Penny? Penny. Terry had it straight now.

"It's Dick, Dick Richard," the voice said, introducing himself as if Terry hadn't been the one to come to this address specifically to see him. "I'm glad you accepted my invitation to come over here to my office this time. I prefer this to entering your place without permission again like the last time we met."

"Ha," replied Terry, humorlessly.

"Now, not to start off on the wrong foot or anything," Dick's voice echoed out of the speaker. "But if you try anything funny, I'll put you six feet under."

Terry knew he had nothing to worry about if it came down to a dick measuring contest with Dick Richard; he had seen the outline of Dick's penis against his pants when he was at Terry's house in the first book, and it was nothing to write home about. "More like six inches," Terry muttered under his breath.

"What was that?" asked Dick. "Never mind. I'll buzz you in, get up here."

The door buzzed annoyingly, and Terry creaked it open and made his way up the scuffed-up staircase and down the dimly lit hall to office 206. The door read:

DICK RICHARD

PRIVATES INVE TIGATOR

Someone had apparently moved the S. The door swung open, the light from a large window opposite the entrance revealing the large and in charge outline of Dick Richard framed in the doorway.

"Well, well," gargled Dick Richard. "If it isn't Terry O'Broadside. Also known as, let's see here, a number of aliases including Thierry de Bordeaux, Larry Broadside, Terrence O'Sideboard, Gary Boardside… and more I'm sure, come in, come in!" Dick Richard turned and walked back toward a desk by the window, waving and beckoning Terry to enter.

Terry followed him into an office that basically matched the rest of the of the descriptions already provided of the building, just with more stacks of poorly arranged papers everywhere. This place could use some organizing. The tips of Terry's fingers tingled as he pictured just what he could do for this place. A week of Terry's services and it wouldn't be half bad, really.

"Seeing anything of interest?" asked Dick Richard, sitting down behind his desk. A wrinkly overcoat covered the back of Dick's chair, and a broad-brimmed hat hung on a hook on the wall. Terry took the seat opposite him. "There wouldn't be anything that could tempt you here in my simple little operation."

Terry glared at the beefy man in front of him. Despite the humble surroundings and the sloppy slob in front of him, Terry knew he was dealing with someone with more than impressive detective skills. This man was a rustic but competently put together pie with a pastry crust completely covering the top. Sure, maybe he wasn't baked perfectly, but who knew what was really inside? "Don't act stupid," Terry said. "You aren't stupid. If you were stupid, and you'd still managed to figure out who I am and all of whatever this is about today, what would that make me? Don't answer that."

"Well let's get down to it then," said Dick. "You're here because I said that magic word, Penny. Well, I've got a tip for you. A really big tip."

Terry scoffed internally at this as well. The tip of Dick's penis was one of the most clearly outlined parts of his penis that Terry had been able to observe through Dick's pants the last time Terry had seen him, and he wouldn't use "really big" to describe it. Weirdly shaped, maybe. Bulbous? Turnip-like? Terry didn't say anything aloud this time though, because he realized he had been thinking a lot about Dick Richard's penis and not a lot about Penny these past few moments.

"So," said Dick. "It seems that Penny has been able to work quickly and take on some new jobs for herself, she's no longer under Peter Zeria's greasy thumb. But according to my tip, her cover has been blown by another agent. She might be in danger, serious danger. All I know is that they were both undercover at a bottled water company, and this other agent, he was able to make quick work of your lady's disguise. For what purpose, I don't know. Maybe Penny was about to find out. But he's a slick operator."

A bottled water company. Water. Wa-ter. Wa-Terry? No, he'd been through this last time. And Wa-Terry just sounded like the name an evil color-swapped version of himself. Now there was an uncomfortable thought, for a number of reasons.

"Why are you telling me this?" asked Terry.

Dick Richard stared hard at Terry for a moment, their eyes locking. "This can be a lonely business. I got a tip. My options were to either sit on this information and do nothing with it. Or to maybe make it a little less lonely. For me, and for you."

Terry was stunned. Dick Richard was as tough as a tough piece of meat, on the outside. But on the inside, might he be as tender as a tender piece of meat? Terry felt like he could see something, deep in Dick's eyes. Was there a deeper Dick? A tingle went up his spine, and he saw Dick almost imperceptibly shiver as well.

"Just kidding!" said Dick Richard, quickly breaking the moment. "It's because I want to have a leg up on you and to have you owe me a favor, if I ever need it! Haw haw haw!" Dick's laughter was something like the braying of a donkey. Not unpleasant, but more at home on a farm.

"Of course," said Terry. He remembered now, Dick Richard was a jackass. Of course.

"Here's what you're going to do. Go seek out Jarlene Bergen next Wednesday at the bottled water company. Best I can tell you she's connected to our man in some way and might have some answers as to what happened to your girlfriend. See what you can find out from her, on the sly. I'll send you the address. Maybe you'll find something useful."

Terry briefly considered shaking hands with Dick, but he didn't see a sink or any hand sanitizer anywhere in the office. So with that, he left.

Chapter 2:
Man on Man

Terry had needed to burn off some energy, so he had walked to his meeting with Dick Richard, and had now walked back home. Terry strolled up to his condo building and entered through the underground parking garage. He passed by his Nissan Cube, sitting seductively in its parking spot in the parking lot. Terry moaned gently, feeling a moment of intense pleasure just at seeing his automobile from a distance. What a beautiful vehicle.

***

Dick Richard also walked home, because he lived like one minute from his office. He walked past his car, a real piece of crap Toyota Echo covered in parking tickets, street parked outside his building. It was barely functional – he had to go to the scrapyard whenever he needed replacement parts, and the inside smelled like animal pee. His last car had been an even older Toyota Echo too. What a terrible vehicle.

***

Terry took the elevator up and entered his condo. Terry's new house companion, a genetically modified hairless cat, stoically looked up at him from her perch on the chair Terry had purchased just for her. He rubbed her warm smooth tummy. "Greetings, Peony," Terry said, as she sat up. He patted her delicately on her head, her pearly skin and sparkling diamond eyes radiating approval.

***

Dick trudged up his stairs and opened his door, and his droopy old bloodhound Tidus greets him at the entrance. "Good boy, Tiddy," cooed Dick, scratching the dog's big funny head. The bloodhound's wrinkles rippled around Dick's hand as he scratched him, his slobbery mouth lolling open and his sad soulful eyes staring at him with love and affection.

***

Terry concluded his business in his spotless bathroom, feeling cleansed, rinsed, and cooled by his bidet. He changed into some loose-fitting linen pajamas (he used to wear silk pajamas, but the excessively sexual feeling of silk all over his body all night had led to some restless sleeps), feeling and smelling as fresh as a recently squeezed lemonade. He settled in for the evening, preparing a light dinner of daikon radish and mochi ice cream.

***

Dick finished taking a dump, and wiped himself with the oddly rough and scratchy cheap bargain toilet paper he always purchased. He threw on a wife beater tank top (he didn't love the name, but he was a big fan of Marlon Brando's performance portraying the main character in A Streetcar Named Desire) and some old basketball shorts, pulling at the already forming wedgie his underwear always ended up in as he walked to the kitchen to microwave some leftover instant noodles.

***

Terry was trying to relax. He was curled up in his cushiest chair, safe at home in his pristine condo, and was reading the new book in Charcute Haggis's *Spooky Snackhouse* series, "Better Off Bread." The series was about a baker from small-town Louisiana who falls in love with a diabetic vampire. In this volume, Spooky had to work on controlling her blood sugar, while also fending off the romantic interests of a sexy wererat who owned the local flour mill. It wasn't working. Despite the thrilling and titillating adventures on the pages before him, he just couldn't focus.

***

Dick couldn't get his body comfortable, even in his usual spot on his worn and well-loved couch and under his coziest Afghan blanket. He lurched up and grabbed his TV remote, the plastic crevices filled with various greasy junk food residues, and flipped on the tube. Sweaty, muscular wrestlers grappled and strained, the weekly televised AWF

106

match about halfway through. Mya Noose was taking on the Nipple Brothers. Normally he loved these brawny feats of acrobatics and strength, combined with flavorful entrances, witty banter, and enticing storylines. But Dick couldn't keep his mind on that either.

***

Terry decided to play with his balls for a bit, which always made him feel better. He took out his set of ceramic, chiming Chinese therapy balls. He rotated them clockwise, then counterclockwise, then switched hands, always making sure the balls never touched each other. He could feel the soothing sensation of his finger bones delicately moving in unison, every tendon and ligament stretching and relaxing. Terry breathed a deep sigh of satisfied relief.

***

Dick decided to play with his balls too, but it really wasn't doing it for him. He got out his electric back massager, activating it and lifting it over his shoulder to it run over his broad, meaty, fairly hairy shoulders. It was a Zeria, not a brand he wanted to be associated with, but they really were the best. He could feel the tension melting out of his muscles, and he huffed a satisfied breath of contentment.

***

107

Terry settled into bed, the edges of the sheets tightly tucked in, reviewing the events of the day. That Dick Richard. That old piece of flattened licorice that had fallen under a rocking chair that a dog might find months later. Who did he think he was, lording his information on Penny over him like that, making him go all the way to that smelly office. He'd show him. He would solve this mystery all on his own!

***

Dick scrunched up in his bed, the sheets twisting around him messily. That Terry whatever his last name was. That cocky little snack cake, covered in frosting, and all those sprinkles. Who did he think he was? Ungrateful sasspot, no appreciation for Dick's superior sleuthing. Well he'd show him. He would make Terry solve this mystery all on his own!

***

If there was one thing Terry and Dick both knew, it was that they were nothing alike and had nothing in common with each other. With that, they both drifted off to sleep.

Chapter 3:
Casting Couch

Terry received a text message with many spelling mistakes in the morning with the location of the bottled water company Dick Richard had mentioned. The contact he was to meet, Jarlene Bergen, was an executive in the bottled milk branch of the business. Terry would need to be at his most clever to glean any useful information from her.

Terry didn't have a job lined up yet this time as cover, what with the short notice and all, so he was here for a job interview instead. He hadn't quite finished up his cover story, but he knew his new alias would be his best one yet. His lack of planning meant he would likely have to rely on his sexuality even more than usual. He was prepared to really turn it on, if needed, and had brushed and flossed his teeth twice and worked out his cheek muscles to deepen his dimples to really ensure his smile was at its most dazzling. He also had on a shirt he had designed and tailored himself. It was perfectly adjusted for his wonderful upper body.

Seated on a couch outside Jarlene's office, he stood up as the door opened. Jarlene poked her head out, looked at Terry, and stepped out into the room. Fiery tresses of burnished bronze hair, eyes of viridescent green. In a flash, Terry recognized her – it was Penny.

Terry was stunned. Penny was indisputably a master of disguise, and he had never once even come close to seeing through one of her costumes. But today he had, right away. There she was. Maybe his recent personal growth had allowed him to overcome this particular weakness?

Jarlene/Penny flashed a brilliant smile Terry's way. The smile hit Terry's eyes and he felt like he had been struck by lightning, his heart pumping faster, his blood flowing powerfully through his veins into all of his extremities, immediately arousing him. "Hi, welcome to the water bottle company. Don't forget to drink a big bottle of water today," Penny said. "And also some milk. If you're here for your interview, then come on in."

Terry stumbled numbly after her, stopping in the middle of the room with his head spinning. Penny closed the door behind them and crisply walked around Terry to stand in front of him. She studied him, head tilted, arms akimbo, one hip cocked to the side, toes pointed outwards in her tall, pointy shoes.

Terry felt compelled to speak. "I'm Barry Toadsi…"

Penny cut him off immediately with a quick gesture. "You're so dependable, Terry! I sent out that little tip and here you are! And now that you're here, let's get down to work. Someone with your… intermediate level of skill will be very valuable for my needs."

Somehow, Terry wasn't surprised. Of course. Of course he hadn't gotten one up on Penny. Was he even here to help her? He sighed inwardly.

"What is this about, Penny?"

"Well, I'm almost ashamed to admit it, but I've run into a small hurdle in my work here. I was undercover here with two different aliases at once, not a stretch for someone as efficient as me. I was Jarlene Bergen, Executive Vice President of Milk and Drinkable Dairy Products. And I was also Oka Boursin, a newly transferred accountant from the company's other office in the Alps. Well, someone compromised that alias somehow. A fairly distressing development, as there weren't even any… extenuating circumstances to speak of."

Terry caught the slight hesitance in her voice.

"Anyway, I realized I needed another set of eyes. Whoever this was, they had some serious abilities. And, there being only one of me, who better than you? So I let that tip slip out to your acquaintance Dick Richard and I knew you'd come running."

Terry considered this. "So is this you asking for help without actually asking for help then?"

"I don't know about that," Penny responded. "But we should talk. There's clearly someone here of exceptional skill. While we get down to it, would you like something to drink? Some water? Some milk? Some milkwater? That's a boutique blend of our water and milk. I can have my secretary bring them in."

Terry knew the importance of remaining hydrated. "I'll have a milkwater please."

Penny rang a bell on her desk, and a discrete assistant came in with two bottled milkwaters, which he opened and handed to Terry and Penny.

Terry took a sip from his bottled milkwater. Refreshing and light, and full of calcium. The secretary withdrew and stood deferentially by the door.

Terry's vision began to go a little funny. Then he started to feel woozy. That secretary… Terry hadn't gotten a good look at him. The secretary had averted his gaze the whole time. And had there been something wrong with the way he had handed out those drinks? Something… sinister?

Terry tried to think back. Yes. He had used his… left hand to hand out those drinks. Terry looked over at where the secretary stood. The secretary faced back at him, standing squarely opposite from Terry as if an image in a mirror. Wait, who was that in front of him? Was Terry looking in a mirror? Was he seeing… himself?

Yes. That man did look almost exactly like him, didn't he?

He managed to turn his head, which felt oddly stiff on his neck, and he could see Penny, passed out on the floor next to him. Terry stumbled to one knee, almost passing out himself.

"I didn't expect to see you here," said a familiar voice. "After all this time. Don't try to get in my way. After all, Terry, I know your middle name."

Terry was paralyzed, terrified. "Don't say it!"

"Don't say what? Don't tell anyone that your middle name is Philand…"

"Dooooon't!!" Terry cried.

Terry reached out an arm but grasped only air. His vision blurred, the room spun, colors filled his eyeballs, and he drifted up into the sky as his body fell to the ground.

And then, for the second time in as many adventures, Terry blacked out.

Chapter 4:
The Secret of Terry

"Peony, it's six minutes past 17 o'clock, and I am just approaching the town of India, Indiana," Terry dictated into his Dictaphone. One hand on the wheel and one hand on the recorder, Terry drank his coffee and took a bite of pie. Even after taking that bite, he couldn't tell what the filling was made of, but it was pie. "Indeed, I'm still uncover with the Sikh Rotary, who appear on the surface to be a charitable organization, but are suspected to actually be a Punjabi spy agency, here in the heart of Turtle Island, sometimes known as North America. If all goes well, I will undercover their infamous deeds. Best I can tell, we're headed in a southeasterly direction and remain far north of the equator."

Terry's North American accent was perfect. He was pleased with how this was all going, elated, with the world blurring and hazing outside his car windows as he careened safely down the road, not caroming even once. What had he to fear? As far as the Sikh Rotary was concerned, he was just a secrete-ery. No, he would not be secreting early from this job.

Terry pulled over from the highway at the nearest rectory, where he was quickly sick rectally

in the most convenient private space he could find.
The rector questioned him but Terry had always
been slick rhetorically, and he flashed the shiny
lettering of his badge, proudly yelling "Eff bee
eye!" at the foolish man. He was hungry again, and
must seek a refectory.

Approaching the seashore of the Indiana Ocean,
Terry surveyed the stores and shops lining the
boardwalk. Next to the Sea Crept Treasury stood
the establishment he was looking for, and he
swerved into the drive-through for the Shark
Eatery. He considered the crow-in-burger, but
instead found himself ordering himself six red
herring and a chocolate cherry. A talkie played on
the Terryvision, a soothing spider rocking chair
gently caressing a napping man. Terry ate, he
smiled, he closed his eyes, the first time he could
remember blinking.

He opened them. There before him was a sexy
attorney: silk, red, hairy. "Terry… seek red airy,"
she said to him, her voice dripping with molasses.
"Pazz, Terry!"

If she was the attorney, then he was the
inspector. But he hardly knew her.

"What?" asked Terry, suddenly anxious. He
could not understand his surroundings.

"Pazz! Seek. Red. Airy!" the attorney
annunciated slowly, her voice still thick and
syrupy.

Terry looked around. He was not in his car. He was in… was this a manual Toyota Echo?

Did he have too many arms?

What… what was?

It was…

"Terry!" He felt a slap on his face. "Wake up!"

Terry opened his eyes a second time, this time in real life. His head felt wooly, and his mouth felt like it was full of cotton.

"No… this car…!" Terry gasped, flinging his arms in front of his face to hide the hideous interior of that phantom vehicle.

"Snap out of it!" said Penny testily, giving him a shake.

Terry's head rattled around on his usually sturdy neck. "No need to be so testy…test tea… testes? Wait, where are we?" Terry took a deep breath, gaining his bearings. He was back in Jarlene Bergen's office.

Penny stood up, dusting herself off. "All my files…" she said to herself, looking around at the clearly ransacked office.

Terry was still taking stock of the situation. Whatever that had been, it was some real unnecessary surrealist shit. Absurdist, even. But despite that being his favorite kind of TV show, Terry had no desire to experience it for himself. Like a representative or deputy of a bishop in the

Catholic church, there were some things he liked to experience vicariously.

"Penny!" said Terry, suddenly remembering his dream. Seek red airy, of course! And something about pads, maybe? "I know who must have slipped us that drug! It was your secretary. And…"

"That man…" interrupted Penny. "I didn't pay attention to him at first. Terry, he looked just like you. Maybe a little taller, slimmer. Something of a sinister glint in his eyes, and the way he used his hands. Backwards, somehow. Wrong. But the resemblance was uncanny."

Terry was just remembering what that secretary, who wasn't really a secretary, had said prior to passing out. And he knew the answer to who that was.

Penny stared at him hard. "Terry, was that some sort of… evil doppelganger?"

"Not an evil doppelganger. At least, I hope not. But someone whose skills have always rivaled my own in almost every way," Terry said. Terry knew he and Penny would need to work together, that he would need her help to see this through. And not just Penny's help. Unfortunately, there was only one other person he could call. One other person with the necessary skills, who Terry felt some kind of connection with.

"We have to call Dick Richard."

Chapter 5:
Twins, Peeks

Dick Richard had arrived pretty quickly, all things considered. He must not have had a lot going on today. Terry had spied Dick Richard getting out of his rusty Toyota Echo, parked next to a fire hydrant, from Penny's office window, and had barely been able to suppress the full body shudder seeing it induced in him. Now Dick, Penny, and Terry were all seated in a rough triangle; Penny behind her hastily tidied desk, Terry primly on a stool, and Dick schlumped into a chair, leaning back and looking at the ceiling.

For all that existed between them, Dick hadn't questioned Terry when Terry had called him and asked him to come. Terry looked at Dick Richard, really looked at this poutine of a man. When it came down to it, Dick was proper, chunky, real potato fries, and thick, rich gravy. Yes, those fries were a little soggy from spending too much time in their take-out box, and yes that gravy was getting cold and starting to congeal. But Terry knew that Dick had the curds where it counted. He wasn't shredded cheddar, he was the real, genuine squeaky cheese.

Terry glanced between his two companions, and finally spoke. "Penny, that man you just saw, the one who was acting as your secretary, is not my evil doppelganger, though he might as well be. His name is Walter. He was my best friend, and my teammate. And he's also my estranged fraternal, but mostly identical, twin brother."

Dick and Penny gasped audibly, clearly shocked by this unexpected twist.

"Now let me tell you a very interesting and exciting story about my past."

***

Terry finished telling the story from the prologue, along with some other necessary details about his childhood and so on.

"And that's the story of how my team handball career came to an end. After that game I never saw Walter again. The next morning he had disappeared, and all traces of him went completely dark. It was my fault. I knew I had driven him away with my unwillingness to share the spotlight, to trust him in those big moments. Losing him is why I gave up my sporting dreams and decided to become a secret agent. It was the only way I could think of to find him, not that I've had any luck."

Dick Richard was indignant. "What? You can't just add a secret brother to your backstory!"

"It just never came up before now. Anyway, Walter went off the grid, and I've been searching for him. But I don't know if him also being a secret agent now too is a coincidence or if he's become some twisted copycat of me. He erased all traces of himself nine years ago, and his actions today are the first I've seen or heard of him since."

Penny cleared her throat. "I've been trying to chase down any rumors of whoever this could have been ever since my other identity was busted. I didn't figure out who he was or his connection to you, Terry, of course. Seems like he's a fast riser up the secret agent rankings. But the kind of jobs he takes… he may have gone dark on the inside too."

"Well," said Terry. "This is why I got into this line of work initially, to find him, bring him back. Apologize. Maybe he needs help? Well, no, probably not, let's not be too optimistic about his intentions. But do we have any idea what he's after?"

"The job I was undercover on that he compromised and the files he took from this office were related to a new bottling plant the company just finished construction on. We're rolling out our new line of athletic, pH balanced, isotonic milkwater. It's going to be in glass bottles, but you can buy a special bottle koozie, sort of like a sock, so they don't shatter on the court. Once we go into production, they'll be delivered to every sports drink drinker's home every morning."

"Then let's return to the scene of the crime he's about to commit," said Dick. "We'll have to do a steak out, find out what he's up to there."

"Don't you mean a stake out?" asked Terry, detecting the spelling of the homonym from the way Dick said it.

"Not the way I do it," said Dick, pulling out a George Foreman grill and two steaks from inside his coat.

"You two go ahead," said Penny. "I'll wait for your signal and try to sneak in through the back of the factory."

"Alright," said Terry. "But Dick, we're using my car. We'll have to walk to go get it."

***

Terry and Dick sat outside the pristine new bottling factory, discretely tucked away in an alley in Terry's perfect automobile, polishing off their medium rare steaks that Dick Richard had expertly prepared on his portable grill. Terry had made sure to put a towel down on Dick's seat, and gave him a whole stack of wet wipes to clean his hands. In the dimming evening light Dick occasionally gazed around appreciatively at the vehicle's sparkling interior.

Terry glanced over at the man next to him. Yes, he was silly, and yes, their paths had crossed previously under somewhat acrimonious circumstances. But Dick had come to help him.

"Listen Dick, I appreciate you being here," Terry offered.

Dick chewed his steak, his mouth a little open as he did so, and answered while still chewing. "Well, I'm not in this business to make enemies. What I really want is to do cool detective stuff, and I figured if I stuck around with you, I'd have some interesting opportunities."

Terry nodded along, understanding. "I have to be honest with you, Dick. When you uncovered my identity, I did some digging into your past, to protect myself. Or at least to ensure some mutual destruction. So… yeah, I found your series of live erotic podcasts you made under various pseudonyms. And I listened to all of them."

Dick briefly stopped chewing. "They were great concepts," Terry continued. "James Bulge, Dangle O Seven. There's nothing wrong with those being out there really. They were actually good. But I know why you had to quit. It's because in that last episode you lost control, and everyone learned that you blurt out confidential information whenever you orgasm. That time specifically, it was the passwords to your various streaming service accounts."

Dick was silent a moment. "I had always dreamed of being an erotic voice actor. But my weakness was one I couldn't work around. Plus, I had so many people logging on to my Netflix after that."

"And that's a weakness I planned to exploit, if I needed to," said Terry. "But… what I'm trying to say is, I don't think I'll need to."

Dick Richard kept chewing, considering all this. Then he smiled broadly and stuck out his hand. "Put 'er there, partner!" he said.

Terry took his hand, squeezing it firmly. "I'm not sure about partner, but…"

"Look!" Dick Richard said, pointing out the window. Sure enough, there was someone that looked an awful lot like Terry sneaking in the front door of the factory.

"Alright," said Terry. "Let's take a little look at what's going on here."

Terry radioed Penny, who confirmed she was on site and would be infiltrating from the rear. Terry and Dick exited the car, and the two of them danced through the shadows, approaching the factory unnoticed. They silently opened the door, peeking into the dark interior for any sign of the man they were after.

The door slammed behind them and lights snapped on, one spotlighting the two intruders, and another illuminating an attractive figure standing in front of them.

"Oho, so my twin appears!" crowed Walter.

Chapter 6:
Second Chances

Terry was facing Walter for the second time today, but in many ways for the first time in years. Walter looked just like Terry in almost every sense, just maybe a little stretched out. They were even dressed alike, except in opposite color pallets.

"Walter… I…" Terry stammered uncharacteristically.

"And now my twin speaks!" laughed Walter, a cruel smile on his face.

Walter stepped forward, the light catching his handsome face. "You thought you were sneaky? You thought I wouldn't feel the raw sexual heat radiating off your Nissan Cube from miles away? I'm in a bottling factory, the resonance of all these glass bottles around me caused the infinitesimally quiet and gentle electric hum of that wonderful beast's Zeria-brand car batteries to resound like thunder!"

Terry didn't necessarily love the Zeria company, but they really did make the best batteries. And he should have known that Walter would be attuned to his car. The two of them had spent countless hours as children looking through the window of the Nissan showroom, hoping to drive one of those manly and mighty Cubes one day.

"Walter, where have you been? What are you doing here, what is this about?" asked Terry. "Is this about…?" Terry began, but he saw Walter's eyes darkening and stopped himself. No. This wasn't about him. It was a coincidence.

"It has nothing to do with YOU, if that's what you were going to ask," Walter sneered. "It's just my luck that the person I needed to steal information from would turn out to be your old girlfriend. Yes, I know all about that. No, I'm here to continue plans that have been years in the making, all on my own! Plans that you have no idea about, and that you won't hear all the details of today! I don't need you, or anyone else on my team. But just so you have a small idea of the big picture, let's just say that the drug I slipped you earlier is just a little taste of what's to come. Yes, this small part of my overarching master plan is to slip this drug into this incredibly popular and delicious new milkwater beverage that will be showing up at every health-conscious person's door tomorrow morning."

Behind Walter the shiny and new bottling machinery stirred to life, conveyor belts moving, pipes and vats rumbling, gauges moving to indicate something was going on. "Yes, it's even the official athletic beverage of the May Mayhem tournament, the collegiate national championship for team handball, the last place we saw one another. There's no way you could comprehend my plans, and there's nothing you can do to stop me! You'll just have to settle for thinking this is all for inscrutably evil purposes."

Was this just another sports-related mystery, in the end? Terry needed to branch out. But no, it couldn't be just that. Walter was working on something bigger, and spreading this psychogenic drug was just one small piece. Walter was also monologuing, and they both knew it. Yes, it would be good to mull this all over later, but this distraction must mean that there actually was a way to stop him.

"You're thinking that you being here will throw a wrench into my plans," Walter crooned. "Don't even think about it. This new bottling plant has undergone so much continuous improvement and had its processes mapped out so efficiently that even throwing a wrench literally into the machinery wouldn't do anything. But maybe you can try to stop me with this."

Walter pulled something out of his back pocket. A regulation-sized handball. Walter smoothly tossed it underhand to Terry, who reflexively caught it.

"Once I knew you were involved, I knew I could bait you here so we could play this little game while my plans came to fruition. Just for fun! I know you. You do have one chance to stop me here, to delay my plans. You have to throw a ball. You can see on the wall behind me that there's a switch. Only this handball can activate it and stop the machine. If you can make the shot, you'll save the day. But you'll have to get through me."

This was Terry's time. Only he could do anything about this situation. An impossible shot? Not for him.

"Forget it Terry!" laughed Walter. "I'm 3 inches taller than you, and you know my wingspan is disproportionately wide!"

Terry looked around. Time was ticking down. He was once again back on the handball court, the game on the line. His memories of all the passes he never made to Walter passed before his eyes. It hadn't mattered then. They had won. Except it had mattered. To Walter. And now look at what had become of him.

Terry considered the situation. Yes, Walter was in the way, and yes Water was taller, a better defender than him really. Those six extra inches in his wingspan would make the difference. Terry did know that. There was no way past him.

So, the height difference. That was one difference between them. Another was apparently that Terry had principles and Walter did not. Terry looked around him. Dick Richard had been sneaking off to the side, creating some space between them. And there, sneaking in from behind

Walter, was Penny. Terry had what most would consider an impossible shot. No one could make that shot… maybe not even Terry. That's why Walter was so confident. But maybe Terry had another difference from Walter. Maybe he had friends.

He again heard the voice of the attorney from his dream. Now he understood. Terry dug deep, deep into that part of him that was always afraid to do so, and trusted some else. He passed.

Faking a shot towards Walter, he instead flipped the ball to Dick Richard, who fumbled it clumsily but came up with the catch. Walter moved to block Dick's view, but Dick threw the ball with surprising force over to Penny. Penny smoothly caught it and dunked it right into the switch, shutting off the machine. The factory went quiet.

"Noooooo!" Walter shouted in a rage. "There's no way that you'd share the glory! How could I have been wrong about that? Arrrrgh! I'll get you next time Terry! This isn't over. And just so you know, my name isn't Walter anymore – you can call me Waterry! Wa-Terry!"

There was a blinding flash of light and smoke, and Walter was gone.

Chapter 7:
The End…?

Terry and Penny sat together on Terry's bed, back in his apartment. It had been a long day. They had succeeded in stopping whatever that was, and they were back in one another's company without any disguises or adventures going on for the first time since back when they'd first met. Back when Terry had fallen for her, hard. Had fallen in love. Penny reached over and put her hand on Terry's. Neither spoke for a minute, before Penny looked up and met his eyes.

"To tell you the truth Terry… it wasn't just you who slipped up when we worked together," Penny began. "I did too. Yes, I left you out to dry, and fulfilled my job by screwing you over, but it affected me too. I made a mistake and got exposed. I did some digging, and it must have been Walter that found whatever thread I left loose and kept on pulling until he had enough for a medium-sized cross stitch pattern. That's how Peter Zeria got ahold of some information on me, and why I was forced into working for him. Walter must have sold him the information to gain something for his plan."

Penny sighed. "Such a large man, that Peter. It wasn't until you threw him off his baseball dreams that I could get myself out from under him. That, and the information on Zeria I stole from Benjamin Bogard. Oh, and some of what I swiped from your drive on your other job before that. So thank you for that. But… what I'm trying to say is… I wasn't… totally immune to the emotional impact of betraying you. It knocked me sideways as well, which I wasn't prepared for, and let this whole situation today happen, what with Walter tracking me down, then me getting you involved."

"Well," said Terry. "It isn't all bad. We did pretty good work together. You and me. And Dick Richard, I guess."

"True enough," replied Penny. "Oh hey, if I were to open that closet, would I find a certain something from the last time you and I saw each oth…"

"Yes," replied Terry quickly and honestly.

Penny gave a brief giggle, then her expression turned serious again. "Listen, I want you to know this. When I first saw you, I didn't know you were undercover. I saw you and I thought, 'Hey, who's that? I want to get to know that guy.' And when we first spoke, I knew we would get along, that we'd immediately be friends. I really felt that deep inside. And as we got to know one another further, even after I found out you were also undercover and that I could use you, I… I really did value our time together." She had felt and thought more than that, of course. But she didn't say it.

Terry could see there was something left unsaid in Penny's eyes. But he didn't prod. He just said, "So did I."

They spent the night together. And in the morning, she was gone.

***

Terry was tired. He was busy gardening in his rooftop plot. The sun hadn't even come up yet. He pruned his squashes. He squashed his prunes. And he thought.

Terry loved being a secret agent, but some mornings he just didn't feel sure what was next. He wasn't sure where this adventure left things, and he definitely hadn't been at his most sharp or proactive. But it had been interesting. And maybe he'd gained something else from it.

Terry wiped sweat from his brow with his forearm, not wanting to touch himself with his dirty gardening gloves. He skillfully handled some oblong vegetables, squeezing them to test their plumpness. Dick, who had spent the night on Terry's carefully covered couch, came up onto the roof through the door to the stairwell.

"So," Dick said, yawning and taking a sip of coffee. "Are we… friends now?"

This case had had more twists than a whole pack of Twizzlers. This certainly wouldn't be the biggest one.

"You might be my only friend," Terry conceded sadly.

"So not just friends, best friends!" Dick said happily.

"Well… I guess that's technically true," Terry replied with a small smile.

Terry wasn't sure where Penny had gone, but they had parted on what he thought were good terms. He wasn't sure where Walter had gone either, or what Walter was planning. But he knew he wouldn't have to face that alone.

Dick sat down in a lawn chair to finish his coffee, while Terry continued gardening. The two of them quietly enjoyed watching the sun rise.

Bonus:

A VERY TERRY CHRISTMAS

A Very Terry Christmas

Christmas was coming, and so was Terry. He was coming over to Dick Richard's office.

Yes, it was almost Christmas, which meant a few things for Terry. It meant his condo had significantly more tinsel hanging from various surfaces than it usually would. It meant snow on the ground, and snowflakes gently drifting down through the air. It meant that all the evergreen trees had balls dangling roundly from their branches. And it generally meant that he would be all alone, usually taking advantage of the holiday break to get in a little extra undercover work, with everyone out of the various office buildings he found himself working at. But this year, it meant he would finally have a chance to win the big holiday charity co-ed three-on-three basketball tournament, which would take place over the next three days leading up to Christmas.

Terry whistled to himself in a Christmassy way while striding down the sidewalk, his two enormous balls bouncing in their sack with his every step. Today was the opening round of the tournament, and he wanted to arrive early to take some practice shots. That's why Terry had a sack of basketballs, so he and Dick could warm up before the game.

Terry had assembled an unbeatable team. Terry would be the captain, and with his long-range accuracy he would be the primary shooting option for the team. Dick Richard would be their big man, playing forward and hopefully taking care of the rebounds and displaying his finishing touch around the hoop. And, in a miraculous turn, Terry had found that Penny had left her phone number in his phone, and, a few texts later, she had agreed to join the team and complete their roster.

One small piece of Penny's backstory that Terry had managed to uncover was that she had been the top university basketball recruit out of high school, and she had more than lived up to her reputation as a feared ballhandler and playmaker in her university days. Her deceptive passes and smooth dribbling had created incredible plays and broken many an ankle. Penny would be the driving force of their team, running their offence. With the three of them combining their skills, there was no way they could lose.

Terry had found several video clips of Penny in action during her playing days, and he reviewed them in his mind while walking. Penny's signature look had been her distinctive red hair, tied up in a flashy top ponytail, and every pass she made was perfection.

Terry was going to pick up Dick at his office, and Penny would join them at the gym. Terry had arrived early and found the door unlocked, and Dick not there, so he had let himself in and taken the time to tidy and clean Dick's office. It was spick and span, it was straight and organized, it was really just much better than it had been before.

Dick's office door opened, and Santa Claus walked in. No, wait, it was just Dick Richard, dressed as Santa Claus.

"Ho ho ho!" said Dick Richard in a jolly, festive way. "Hey, this place looks fantastic! Let me get changed out of this Santa Claus outfit, then let's grab a bite to eat at this great place I know before we head to the gym."

They stopped by a little hole in the wall spot and the food was delicious, the kind of grilled meat skewer in a wrap with all kinds of stuff type of food you were sure would disagree with you tomorrow, but that you ate every time anyway. They even had a special Christmas meat, turkey, that was topped with cranberry sauce and gravy.

Feeling fueled up and comfortably full, the pair headed to the gym.

***

Penny was late. Terry nervously fiddled with the strap of his uniform top, the straps spanning his strong collar bones, held up by his ample trapezius muscles and showing off his round and defined deltoids. Their team was called the Dunking Donairs, and their uniforms were white with neon orange and pink trim. The rosters for the tournament were strictly set, and Terry hadn't registered any subs, not knowing anyone else who would want to play, but also not thinking it would be necessary.

Their opponents, the Chiseley Bears, were known to be a particularly strong and physical team that spent more time lifting weights than practicing basketball. Terry eyed them down on the other side of the court, while trying not to glance too often at the door to see if Penny would arrive. Terry's own bare arms were no less impressive than theirs, but they did look large and intimidating in their dark brown uniform kits. They would need Penny's skills to win today and move on in the tournament.

The doors opened and there she was, in her team uniform and with her bright red hair up in a ponytail above her… thickly muscled and hairy body? Penny had a strong physique but this was… wait, was that Benjamin Bogard, wearing a Penny wig?

Benjamin jogged over to Terry and Dick. "Sorry guys, Penny couldn't make it, so she sent me in her place. I'm Penny today. She figured I owed you an apology. It wasn't your fault, what went down at my company in the first book, and I shouldn't have tried to blackmail you. She also reminded me that you damaged the Zeria company's reputation badly with all that baseball stuff. So here I am. Let's basketball!"

The officials didn't look twice at Benjamin as they verified the team rosters. The whistle blew, Dick took the tip-off, and the game began.

***

It was the next day, and the air was even Christmassier than ever. Random groups of people were on every street corner singing Christmas carols, and Terry could almost hear sleighbells with every step he took.

Terry thought back to last night's game. Benjamin had been no replacement for Penny as a playmaker, but his brawniness and physicality in combination with Dick Richard had greatly helped them drive to the net and create some space in the key, not to mention all the fouls they had drawn. Absent Penny's abilities, Benjamin had been the exact player they had needed to overcome their opponents. He and Terry had shaken hands at the end of the night and parted ways without animosity.

One win down, two to go.

Penny was late again, and Terry hadn't heard from her, despite trying to text her the day before. Tonight was the semi-finals, and they were playing the Stretchymoes, a particularly tall team whose motto was "tall is all." They weren't the most skilled, but they had the height and made it count.

Terry could see them warming up, all of them easily able to touch the backboard in their light blue uniforms. They would definitely need Penny today to make it to the finals. Where was she?

But wait, the doors opened and there she was, with that same hair and this time with her normal body… but hang on, that wasn't Penny's face. Was that… Annie Kometz, the fake reporter undercover agent, wearing Penny's uniform and the same Penny wig? Or was her name Pepper O'Neil, who had been a baseball agent, and also an undercover agent?

Annie, or was it Pepper, hustled over to Terry and Dick. "Sorry guys, Penny couldn't make it, so I'm here as Penny instead. She figured I owed you, for trying to kill you in the second book. We're old colleagues from our time working for Peter Zeria. And she got me out on bail to participate in this charity event, so I owe her too. Plus, I'm not such a bad basketball player myself."

"Okay, whatever," Terry said. "Wait, did we ever get a real name for you?"

"Nope. My real name is Stephanie Cooper," she replied.

"Stephanie Cooper. Is there… is there a pun there?" Terry asked.

"No, it's just a normal name. Anyway, let's play ball."

Jump ball at center court, and the game was underway.

***

Christmas Eve. The Christmas spirit was reaching a feverish zenith. The temperatures were reaching a frosty nadir. Every pole Terry saw reminded him of the North Pole, and Santa who would soon be on his way.

Last night had gone well too. Stephanie's skill with the hook shot and in setting up alley oops had really helped them to overcome their height deficiency. She had even given Terry her number, but despite her value to the team and Terry not holding a grudge over their previous encounter, he wasn't sure he'd ever call it.

Two wins down, one to go. It was down to the championship game.

"She's late again, again," said Terry.

"Well, hopefully she shows up," said Dick Richard. "Or if she doesn't, hopefully she sends someone else in her place again. Wait, this is the third game, who owes you a favor from the third book?"

There wasn't really anybody, not with Walter having been set up as the likely antagonist of any potential future installments. They would need somebody, though. The opposing team, the Bad Guys, dressed all in black, were running drills for their unique only lay-ups style of play across the gym.

But then, there she was. This was assuredly the real Penny, finally joining them. Her uniform, her distinctive red hair and ponytail, her body, her face… but wait… she was standing there sort of stiffly. Was that just the realistic sex doll from the first book, that Terry had been keeping in his closet?

Terry and Dick went and retrieved the anatomically correct mannequin and brought her to their end of the court. "I haven't looked for this since I last saw Penny," said Terry. "Did she take it from my closet? Must be where the wig came from. I guess this will have to be our third player tonight."

They set the doll up in their half of the court, and got ready to ball.

***

Terry and Dick were walking down the sidewalk, snow falling quietly, their footsteps almost inaudible, all sound muted by the thick covering of snow. Red and green lights softly lit their path, illuminating the winter wonderland around them. Terry had the sex doll under his arm. Dick had their trophy held in both his hands. The doll had turned out to be a surprisingly effective defender.

"I'm sorry she never actually showed up," Dick said.

"Me too," said Terry. They had reached Dick's apartment, which was on the way to Terry's place from the gym. "Still, not a bad result, all things considered. Want to join me back at my place for an eggnog, or perhaps an oatnog?"

"Sure, let me just drop off our trophy and get the pup," Dick replied.

With Tidus retrieved, they walked back to Terry's place companionably, the dog pulling on his leash and sniffing eagerly as they went.

Terry let them in to his apartment, a cozy fire going in his artificial fireplace. Dick let Tidus off the leash, and he and Peony respectfully sniffed each other before curling up together on a pillow in front of the fire.

Terry opened his fridge and got out the eggnog and the oatnog, stored next to the many cases of the new athletic milkwater he always kept on hand. That wonderful beverage had kept the team hydrated and energized throughout the tournament.

He poured their drinks into some glasses and Terry and Dick exchanged gifts. Terry had gotten Dick a snazzy new trench coat, accurately measured to fit his frame like a golf glove, instead of like a baseball glove like his old one. Dick had gotten Terry a whole set of scale model Nissan Cubes and a racetrack for them.

There was a knock on the door, and Terry went to answer it. There was no one in the hall, but right outside his door sat a large, giftwrapped box, with *"To Terry, Love Penny"* scrawled on a small tag.

Terry dragged it into his home and opened it. Despite the large and heavy box, inside was just a Christmas card and a USB thumb drive with a folded post-it note on it. Terry opened the card first. Written inside was:

Sorry I couldn't be there in person. I hope the replacements I sent were adequate. And maybe this will make up for it. xoxo

Terry picked up the thumb drive and read the post-it note. It just read *"Walter."*

"What is it?" Dick asked.

"It's a plot device, to get us started on our next adventure," Terry replied.

Terry's pleasant, digital cuckoo clock chimed as the hands struck midnight. The faintest sound of reindeer hooves could be heard on the roof.

"Merry Christmas, Dick," Terry said to his teammate and friend.

Dick smiled back. "Merry Christmas, Terry."

Secret Terry will return! Maybe. Unless…?

Available on Amazon and Kindle Unlimited

In **Cold Cut,** a mistake from Terry's past reveals his identity and threatens to blow his cover for good. But when a chance to get even for this betrayal presents itself, Terry dives back into the world of high stakes corporate espionage. The one problem is… the person he's up against might also be his one true love!

In **Dead Battery**, Terry swings into the dirty underbelly of professional baseball, where a routine investigation into possible rampant steroid use quickly turns into a murder investigation. Will Terry be able to unravel the mystery and find the killer, or will he be the next one taken out at the ballgame?

In **Six Inches**, a man as secretive as Terry has few friends, but Terry finds himself in need of help when a mysterious new nemesis threatens all that he holds dear. He'll have to team up with old rivals and former lovers if he wants to survive, but can anyone defeat a villain who seems to be as handsome and amazing as Terry himself?

About the Authors

Horatio Quan and Daphne McGuire are newlywed writing partners. They have continued writing while on an extended honeymoon visiting the capitals of the European Union in alphabetical order, and plan to coparent several human babies and multiple dogs on an organic avocado farm. The Secret Terry series is their first work of fiction.

www.ingramcontent.com/pod-product-compliance
Lightning Source LLC
Chambersburg PA
CBHW031254060726
47590CB00003B/898